The Flames of Lilly Pilly Creek

Abbie L. Martin

Book 4 - A Lilly Pilly Creek Ghost Mystery

THE FLAMES OF LILLY PILLY CREEK

ISBN: 978-0-6457139-7-8
Abbie L. Martin Paperback edition / October 2024
Abbie L. Martin books are published by Abbie Allen Publishing

CHAPTER 1

A woman wearing a short red jumpsuit was floating upside down above a kitchen table, her auburn locks dangling. A second woman, her brown hair pulled into a high ponytail, sat at the table, staring at a laptop, pressing buttons and typing.

"Autumn." The woman lifted her head from the computer. "Couldn't you at least try to be helpful?"

"Jones, you know I can't use a laptop," Autumn replied. She remained upside down her arms at her side, legs flipping and kicking.

"What on earth are you doing?"

"Irish dancing," said Autumn. Her tone implied this should have been obvious. Jones sighed. She didn't bat an eyelid at her sister suspended upside down in mid-air. The novelty of Autumn now existing as a ghost was starting to wear off. Yes, she may be dead, but to Jones Autumn was also just her sister. And whilst she was utterly thrilled to have her back, it didn't make them any less sisters. Sisters who annoyed and entertained each other in equal measure.

"Not particularly helpful in the event of a bushfire," said Jones.

"What bushfire?" asked Autumn.

"The one we're preparing this bushfire plan for!" Jones shook her head, resuming her typing. "It says that when the fire is coming, we should wet towels and put them at the bottom of the doors. But we only have hand towels at The Memory Bank."

"We'd better bring some across this morning," said Autumn.

Jones nodded. She picked up a pen and jotted this down on the notepad next to her.

"Did you write down the boxes of water?" asked Autumn.

"Yep," said Jones, clicking the mouse before leaning back in her chair. "I think this is ready to print."

Jones had spent breakfast time preparing their bushfire plan. In three days there was forecasted catastrophic bushfire weather, and living in the Adelaide Hills which was prone to severe bushfires, they needed to be ready.

Autumn finished her jig with a final kick, causing her to flip upright. She grinned and smoothly made her way back down to ground level.

"It's getting serious, isn't it," Autumn said.

"The prospect of a bushfire?" asked Jones. "It certainly seems so. Do you remember the town being this anxious?"

Autumn frowned. "I can't," she replied. "I know every year people talk a lot about getting prepared for bushfire season, but from what I've heard this past week, it seems people believe it's almost inevitable this year."

Jones closed her laptop and, pushing her chair back, rose from the kitchen table. She picked up the notebook and her phone and made her way to the kitchen island where she placed the items into her handbag. Today Jones wore a pale blue t-shirt with the quote "A life lived in fear is a life half lived," from Strictly Ballroom, and the choice was only partially accidental.

This was Jones's first bushfire season in Lilly Pilly Creek for many years. Normally she would be in Adelaide, working as a journalist for

The Advertiser, the number one newspaper in South Australia. However, this summer she was back in Lilly Pilly Creek, having taken over running the family business, The Memory Bank, after her sister's death.

The Memory Bank, a stationery come bookshop come gift store, was a favourite throughout the Adelaide Hills. Visitors even made a point of travelling from Adelaide and throughout South Australia to visit not only The Memory Bank, but Hugo's Wine Bar next door. Lilly Pilly Creek was becoming quite the destination. However, the most unique feature of The Memory Bank was the fact that they had repurposed the old safety deposit boxes as lockboxes for customers to store their memories.

Today, Jones was going to be making the most of this facility. She was planning on placing some of her family's own memories, photos, journals, diaries, letters, and other paperwork, into a lockbox she had recently set up for herself. The sister's felt these items would be safer at The Memory Bank, rather than the family home, in the event a bushfire did breach the town.

"So remind me," said Jones. "I've put everything in the car that I need for the lockbox, right?"

"Yep," said Autumn. "All the important stuff is ready to go."

"I don't know what I'd do if this place burnt down," said Jones, glancing around the kitchen of their childhood home.

"I know what you mean," said Autumn. "I'm thankful for The Memory Bank. Having a solid old bank building with thick walls to protect things is a blessing. But it does remind you how fragile this house would be if a fire came through."

"At least it's a stone house too," said Jones. "Not like some of the weatherboards down the road."

Jones now lived by herself in the family home. It had been in the Eldershaw family for several generations. A gorgeous old stone home, surrounded by a cottage garden that Jones was slowly bringing back to life, in honour of her late mum. Since Autumn's death, she was the only one left in the family. Both their parents had died, and her dad's parents, who had also brought up their family in the house, were no longer with them. It was only Jones. Well, except for the fact that Autumn had returned as a ghost. But that was an entirely different topic.

"You do know The Memory Bank has a generator? Right?"

"Really? Where?"

"I think it's outside, on the far wall," said Autumn.

"Does it still work?"

Autumn shrugged. "I don't know, but I do remember having someone come into service it every twelve months or so. It might be worth checking at some point."

"I have no idea how to start a generator."

"That's what I'm here for!" Autumn twirled, grinning. "But you'd better get cracking if you're stopping at the Lilly Pilly Pantry on the way."

Jones glanced at her watch. "Crap," said Jones. "And don't forget Sybil's."

They both laughed, knowing Jones would never in a million years forget to stop for her morning coffee at Sybil's coffee van.

Jones grabbed her handbag, put on her sunglasses, and made her way out of the house. Autumn, who had zoomed past her, directly through the front door, was already sitting in the passenger seat of Jones's cream Mini Cooper.

"You seem out of sorts," said Autumn, as Jones buckled herself in and started the car.

"Do I?" Jones glanced at her sister, raising her eyebrows.

"Yes, you do."

Jones reversed out of the driveway and onto Lemon Myrtle Street. She sighed.

"I think I'm feeling anxious about the weather and the bushfires," said Jones before smiling. "And don't forget, I haven't had my first coffee yet!"

Autumn laughed. "But is that all?"

"What do you mean?"

"Could it have anything to do with who's arriving in town today?"

"What? Oh you mean Hugo's friends?" Jones kept her eyes on the road.

"Yes," said Autumn. "You've never met anyone from his past. You'd be fine to feel a bit nervous."

Jones didn't respond. She didn't want to admit her sister was right. The thought of meeting Hugo's friends was causing her some concern. She didn't know much about them or how they met, but when Hugo spoke of them, she could tell how important they were to him. They were the people he spent Christmas with when he couldn't spend it

5

with his family. They were important to him, and that meant they were important to her. What would they think of her? Would she be accepted into the group? She didn't know if any of them had wives or girlfriends, but if they did, Hugo hadn't mentioned them. Would they welcome Jones into the fold? And if they didn't, where did that leave her?

Jones pulled the car to a stop next to Sybil's coffee van and turned to her sister. "Perhaps I am a little nervous about that. But I've got nothing to worry about, right?"

"Right," Autumn smiled at her sister, tentatively reaching out her translucent arm, resting it on Jones's forearm, even though she knew she couldn't feel a thing.

Jones smiled back. "I can handle anything as long as I've had my coffee!" She pulled open the car door.

Autumn slid through her door before responding. "Maybe a double shot today!".

CHAPTER 2

"Surely it's too hot for your regular?" called Sybil when she spotted Jones walking up to the van. They noticed Sybil was pouring milk into two cups filled with ice and coffee. The ginger tail of Frank the cat could be seen dangling from a basket, high up on a shelf.

"Absolutely not," said Jones. "It would have to be pretty darn hot for me not to order my flat white. But a double shot please."

If today wasn't hot enough for Jones to change her order, then it would likely never be. The heat was already radiating off the footpath they were standing on, and there was not a hint of cool in the breeze that was rustling the leaves of the gum trees nearby. Jones glanced around, not forgetting the bushfire plan she had prepared that morning, unsure of what the day and week would bring.

"Trixie! Two iced coffees!" A woman with a silvery swept-back bob, wearing tweed pants and a cream blouse, stepped up and grabbed the drinks. Jones was next.

Sybil didn't need to ask Jones for her order. She knew Jones ordered a flat white every morning, and usually more than one a day.

"How are things, Sybil?"

"All good here," said Sybil. "But everyone is worried about the weather."

"I know. It's probably going to be a catastrophic rating on Thursday, right?" asked Jones.

"That's what they're saying." Sybil pressed the coffee machine and the precious brown liquid poured into the takeaway coffee cup.

"I was just working on our bushfire plan this morning," said Jones. "I have a stockpile of towels in the car."

"Towels?"

"Apparently that's what you need if a fire comes through." Jones shrugged.

"Whatever for?"

"You wet them and put them under the doors and on window sills. I guess to stop smoke and heat," Jones explained.

"Well, I don't plan to be here if a fire comes through," said Sybil.

"Are you going to leave Lilly Pilly Creek on Thursday?"

"I think I'll have to," said Sybil. "If a fire comes through this baby has no chance." Sybill tapped the counter of her beloved coffee van.

"We cannot lose Sybil's coffee van!" Jones's eyes were wide at the thought. Sybil twisted a dial and steam hissed as she frothed the milk.

"What will *you* do?" asked Sybil.

Autumn, who was leaning on the van, raised her eyebrows at Jones. Jones knew people may not approve of her plan, but there was no possible way she could leave Autumn. "I'll stay in The Memory Bank," she explained. "I've got all my important things from home in the car. I'll put those in a lock box, and if the fire comes through, I'll just hunker down."

Sybil nodded, not attempting to dissuade Jones, as she swirled the milk into a paper cup before pushing a black lid on top. "Well, I suppose The Memory Bank is the best place to be in Lilly Pilly Creek if a fire does come through."

"I believe so," said Jones, taking her coffee. "Thanks as always,

Sybil!" Jones took a tentative sip of the hot beverage, smiled at Sybil and waved goodbye.

"Really?" said Autumn, as they both returned to the Mini.

"Really what?" asked Jones as she placed the hot coffee into the holder next to her and clipped on her seatbelt.

"Are you really going to stay at The Memory Bank?"

"Of course I am," said Jones, starting the car and moving back onto the road. "How could you ask me that?"

"Ah, because you could be killed!"

"Would that be so bad?" Jones didn't take her eyes off the road.

Autumn gasped, her mouth gaping. "What are you saying?"

"Well, we could be ghosts together," Jones shrugged as she drove down Main Street. She turned right and parked on the side street directly next to The Lilly Pilly Pantry. If she was going to lug boxes of water to the car, she wanted it to be easy.

"You're not serious? Are you?"

"Not really," said Jones. "I mean the thought had crossed my mind. But you don't think The Memory Bank could burn down in a fire, do you?"

"I have no idea!" said Autumn. "Are you really going to risk it? I mean it's one thing to be prepared for a surprise fire, but not when we're being warned days in advance."

"Are you telling me you want me to leave? To leave you?" Jones opened her door as Autumn slid rapidly through the roof.

"Just until the threat reduces," said Autumn. "You know I'll be right here waiting for you."

"You don't know that," said Jones, making her way towards the Lilly Pilly Pantry.

"Of course, I'll still be here!"

Jones glared at her sister as she pushed open the shop door, a bell ringing in the distance. She couldn't reply to her sister. No one else could see Autumn, and she didn't want to get the reputation for being the village crazy lady.

"You can't honestly think a fire is going to hurt me?" Autumn persisted. She hovered in front of Jones who was searching for the water boxes. She couldn't find them in their usual spot.

"I hope they aren't out of water," she muttered.

Autumn flew up in the air, peering out over the top of all the shelves. "They're on a pallet near the front counter."

"Thank you," Jones said quietly, heading to the counter. There stood old Mr Kwok. He never looked all that impressed that customers came into the shop. But Jones had come to know that it was just his resting face. His real personality was jovial, and welcoming, and you could almost call him a rascal.

"What are you after today, Jones?"

"The boxes of water, please Mr Kwok."

"Ah yes, they are proving rather popular," he said. "It's like everyone is preparing for doomsday." Walking out from behind the counter, he grabbed a sack truck that he had ready for just these purchases. "How many would you like?"

"Oh, two please," Jones said. "If that's ok?"

"Not a problem," he said. "I've given everyone a limit of four boxes, but of course, I know a few people have come back for seconds."

"Do you think we need that much water?" Jones's eyes widened. Maybe she wasn't as prepared as she thought.

"Me? Nah. I think everyone's overreacting," he said. "Not the first time we've had a catastrophic day."

"But don't you think this feels different?"

"I think everyone is panicking," said Mr Kwok. "But it is better to be safe than sorry, I suppose."

He loaded two boxes up onto the sack truck and then returned to the counter so Jones could pay.

"What are you planning to do, on Thursday?" Jones asked him.

"I want to stay," he said. "But I don't think the Mrs is going to let me."

Jones nodded. "I'm planning on staying."

"You are?" he said. "I thought I was the only stupid one in town."

Jones laughed at that, although realised she should probably take offence. "Nope! I'm just presuming The Memory Bank is strong enough to withstand a fire. I'd be horrified if anything happened to the lockboxes."

Mr Kwok held out the machine for Jones to pay. "I think they'll be right," he assured her. Jones smiled as her payment beeped.

"I hope you're right," she said, turning back to the water boxes on the sack truck. She wasn't sure if he expected her to push them out to the car, but she needn't have worried. Mr Kwok grabbed the sack truck and indicated to Jones to lead the way.

After he had placed them both in the boot and slammed it shut, Jones thanked him. "Now I just have to get them out myself!" she said with a laugh.

"Keep safe Jones!" said Mr Kwok.

At that moment, the Lilly Pilly Creek fire bell began to bellow.

CHAPTER 3

"It's so loud," moaned Autumn, her hands over her ears.

Jones had pulled up in front of The Memory Bank and was unlocking the wooden front door.

"I just hope it's not close," she said. As she turned to start bringing in all the items from the car, her phone buzzed.

"Hi Atlas, all ok?"

"Well, I've just been called out to my first fire," he responded.

"Oh right, the fire alarm," said Jones, her hand held firmly over her opposite ear attempting to drown out the sound.

"Yep," said Atlas. "Look, I've tried to let clients know, but just in case anyone arrives at The Memory Bank, I wanted to make you aware."

"No problem. I'll handle it. They'll understand, "said Jones. "I hope it's an easy job. Be safe."

Jones ended the call and turned to her car.

"Can you believe Atlas is off to fight his first fire," said Autumn.

Jones grabbed one of the boxes of water and used it to prop open the door. She then grabbed the second one and, huffing and puffing, lugged it to the circular counter in the middle of the main shop area.

"If I'm honest, I'm a bit worried for him," said Jones. "I can only imagine what his mum would be feeling."

"Surely they keep the newbies well out of the way,' said Autumn.

Jones returned to the car and grabbed a box of the items she was planning to place in their lockbox.

"I certainly hope so!"

Although Jones had only known Atlas for a few months, she considered him family. Ever since she had decided to reopen The Memory Bank, after Autumn appeared to her as a ghost, Atlas had been by her side. He'd helped her with everything from the renovations, digitising their records and serving customers, not to mention helping to solve a few crimes. Now that he was volunteering with the Country Fire Service, which everyone called the CFS, she couldn't help but worry for his safety. Every time those women and men put on their helmets and orange uniforms and headed out to a fire, they put their own safety at risk to protect the community. She knew the Adelaide Hills was indebted to them all, and the whole community just wanted to know that every member of the CFS returned home safely.

"Well, there's nothing we can do," said Autumn. "Except ensure we have everything in order here."

"It would have been nice to have Atlas help lug all of this in though." Jones grinned at her sister, as she placed the box on the central counter.

"Why don't you see if Hugo's in?"

Jones shook her head. "No, I don't want to disturb him. I'm sure he's getting ready for his friends to arrive." Back at the car, Jones grabbed the bag of towels and a few other items she had thrown in.

"What does he have to prepare?" Autumn scoffed. "He has a bar full of beer and wine. What more could Hugo's mates want?"

Jones smiled. She had no idea what to expect of Hugo's friends, but Autumn was right. Who wouldn't want a friend who owned a wine bar? Who wouldn't want a *boyfriend* who owned a wine bar, for that matter?

Dumping the bag of towels into the bathroom, Jones turned to the mirror, staring at her red cheeks and the sweat already beading on her forehead. Spinning the cold water tap, she cupped her hands under the cool stream before splashing it all over her face.

"It's not that hot!" said Autumn, gliding into the bathroom.

"How on earth would you know?" said Jones. "You're a ghost. Perfect temperature at all times. Am I right?"

Autumn laughed and shrugged. "If no temperature at all is perfect, then you're right."

"No temperature at all?" Jones turned to her sister and tilted her head. "Really?"

"That's the only way I can describe it," said Autumn. "I don't *feel* anything, not even temperature."

"How strange," said Jones, making her way back to the front door for the second box of water.

"Do you remember that time I waved my hand through the candle flame?" asked Autumn. Jones nodded. "I felt absolutely nothing. I think that's a pretty good test."

"I guess so," said Jones. "Still hard to imagine."

Jones pushed the second water box propping up the door into the room and then paused.

"Can you smell smoke," she said, before turning to look outside.

Jones glanced at Autumn who rolled her eyes. Of course, she

couldn't *smell* smoke.

"But I can try and see where it's coming from." With that, Autumn shot straight up into the air, directly through The Memory Bank ceiling. Jones could only imagine what it must look like from the outside, seeing the red-headed woman burst through the roof, flying above it. That was if anyone other than Jones could see the ghost of Autumn.

It was only a few seconds before her sister returned.

"I can see smoke coming from the west," said Autumn. "I think you might be able to see it from the back."

Jones made her way to the glass doors that opened out onto the new Memory Bank garden. The garden was their pride and joy. Unfortunately, the landscape gardener who had helped to install it, Lorne Fox, had recently been murdered. But his daughter Flick had been instrumental in creating their new oasis, and despite the traumatic circumstances, she had now become one of Jones's friends.

They could hear sirens in the distance, fire trucks making their way to the blaze. The pair moved through the garden and out the back fence. Standing on stubble that had fortunately been mown recently by the council, they looked out beyond the gum trees that lined Lilly Pilly Creek. Jones could just see brownish-grey smoke above the treeline.

"It's not close, is it?" Jones frowned and turned to Autumn.

Autumn shook her head. "No, from what I could see it was a long way away, and it doesn't look like the wind is moving in this direction."

"I know we're prepared," said Jones. "But it still makes me

nervous. Being able to see smoke from the back of The Memory Bank."

"You know you don't have to stay," said Autumn.

"I'm not having the conversation again," said Jones. She turned to walk back into the Bank, knowing customers could arrive at any moment. A strange noise made her stop.

It started as a low rumbling in the distance. Jones felt her chest tense. Is this what a raging bushfire sounded like? She spun back to look at the river, but nothing had changed. The noise got louder and louder until it felt as though the roaring was going to come straight through The Memory Bank. Then it stopped.

"Motorbikes!" called Autumn, who had flown up above the Bank to take a look.

Hugo's friends had arrived.

CHAPTER 4

The morning was spent serving the few customers who came in and checking the CFS website for updates on the fire. There were many fire resources on-site and even an aerial water bomber was being used. The good news was it didn't seem to be moving too quickly, and the longer the day went on the safer Jones felt.

Although Jones was tempted to pop into Hugo's for lunch, just to get a glimpse of his friends, she didn't want to overstep. They had planned to meet for dinner, and that was what Jones would do. Instead, just after eleven, she put the 'back in 15 minutes' sign on The Memory Bank's front door and walked to Sybil's van to pick up one of her iced coffees and a cold piece of zucchini slice. She left Autumn at The Memory Bank who was floating high above the roof line, keeping her eye on the fire.

As she walked, Jones noticed the sharp scent of smoke. It was amazing how it travelled so far. The air was hazy, and the day was climbing to its peak temperature.

"Do you know if they have the fire under control?" Jones asked Sybil as she waited for her extra large iced coffee. Although she would never start her day with anything but a flat white, at lunchtime today a cold beverage was in order.

Sybil shook her head. "I haven't heard anything," she said. "So I'm taking that as no. All hands are still on deck I believe. Otherwise at least one of the firefighters would have come past to grab an iced coffee by now."

"Atlas is out there, you know?"

"Is he?" Sybil's eyes met Jones's. "His first fire?"

Jones nodded. "I'm a bit worried about him."

"They'll keep him safe. Candace the Captain is very good at her job. The crew will look after him." Sybil handed Jones her coffee.

Jones took a sip, and then paused, sighing. It was hard to just stand back and wait whilst one of her friends was putting his life on the line.

"Did I hear a load of motorbikes come into town earlier?"

"Hugo's friends,' Jones explained.

"I heard a rumour they were visiting,' said Sybil. "Have you met them yet?"

"Nope," said Jones. "We're having dinner tonight. I have no idea what to expect."

"I have to say I didn't think Hugo's friends would be bikies!"

"Bikies!" Jones's eyes went wide. "You mean actual bikies?"

Sybil laughed. "No, no don't panic Jones. I don't mean like that. I just mean Harley-riding leather-wearing blokes. I wouldn't have picked it of Hugo."

"I don't know anything about them. I don't even know if Hugo rides motorbikes," Jones said. She furrowed her brow and sipped her coffee. Should she know more about her boyfriend than she did?

"Oh, I like the mysterious types," said Sybil.

"Mysterious types?"

"I just think behind those brown eyes and stubble there's a lot we don't know about Hugo Gilbertson." Sybil was smiling as she handed

Jones a paper bag containing her zucchini slice. Yet Sybil's comments were making Jones feel rather ill at ease. Mysterious? Bikies? Maybe the person she was seeing was someone completely different to who she'd imagined.

A car pulled up and, leaving the car running with the aircon full blast, a young mum jumped out of the car. "Sybil, I am in desperate need of an iced coffee!"

Jones took that as her signal to depart. It was too hot to stand there much longer anyway, and Jones wasn't enjoying the smoky air surrounding them. Making her way back to The Memory Bank, Jones tried her best not to overthink Sybil's words. Of course, she didn't know everything about Hugo. They'd only known each other for a few months and were only a very new couple. They had a lot to learn about each other.

But what if what she learnt about him was something she didn't like? And vice versa for that matter. Memories of failed relationships flashed into her mind. At what stage did the rose-coloured glasses come off? And when you began to learn the depths of another person, how did you know if the way was too murky to continue?

Jones rubbed her eyes. What was with her today? She certainly felt as if she'd woken up on the wrong side of the bed this morning. Was it the layer of concern over the town with the prospect of bushfires? Was it meeting Hugo's friends? Or was it something else she couldn't yet put her finger on?

All she knew for certain was the iced coffee in her hand was just what she needed. She took a long sip from the straw.

Main Street was quiet, almost eerily so. She knew it was because it was simply too hot to be venturing outside. A few people were going in and out of the Lilly Pilly Pantry. There were some cars parked in front of Wren's office and further down near Mr Manowski's, so they were busy with clients. As she walked past Hugo's she saw a few tables of lunchtime patrons no doubt enjoying the air conditioning inside.

Jones pulled her sign off the door and opened up. It was deliciously cool inside, and she thoroughly appreciated the thick stone walls the Bank was made of.

"Autumn! Any updates?" Jones called.

She strode to one of the customer tables and sat down with her coffee and lunch. She'd told Sybil not to heat the zucchini slice. On a day like today, it was perfect cold. Taking a large bite, she relished the savoury egg just as Autumn flew into view.

"A lot of smoke out there," she said. "But it doesn't appear to be getting any closer. You should have seen how high I got!"

Jones paused mid-bite, looking up at Autumn. In her mind's eye, she saw Autumn spiralling up into the sky, bursting through the atmosphere and out into space.

"What?" Autumn laughed, noticing the strange look on her sister's face. "What's the matter?"

Jones swallowed before asking. "How far did you go? How far *can* you go?"

"Pretty high it turns out," said Autumn. "I could see over the first line of hills behind Lilly Pilly Creek at least."

"Ok," Jones sighed. "That seems reasonable. Could you see any flames?"

"No," said Autumn. "A lot of smoke but no flames. Do you think that's a good sign?"

"I guess so," said Jones. "It at least would indicate it's not getting close to us."

"I don't think it is," said Autumn. "But it does feel weird, doesn't it?"

Jones agreed. "I can only imagine what it would feel like if a fire arrived on Lilly Pilly Creek's doorstep."

The thought made Jones shiver.

CHAPTER 5

The afternoon was particularly quiet. Everyone would have been staying inside due to not only the heat, but the smoke, and the prospect of the fire coming their way. Fortunately, it didn't, and just as Jones locked the front door at five that afternoon, an alert popped up on her phone to say the fire had been contained. No doubt the CFS would still be taking shifts throughout the night to ensure no spot fires flared up, but the main danger had passed.

"Time to meet Hugo's friends," Autumn almost sang, as the pair made their way to the wine bar. "Nervous?"

"Of course I'm nervous!" said Jones.

They noticed three large motorbikes parked on the road. Each piled up as though they were travelling the long way round Australia.

"Well, of course, you're nervous," said Autumn. "But you have nothing to worry about. They'll love you. And if they don't, they're idiots."

Jones laughed at Autumn's bluntness. She supposed she was right. It didn't cause the pounding in her chest to disperse though.

As they walked in, they saw several people perched up at the bar or sitting in the booths, enjoying cold pints of beer or glasses of wine. Jones didn't immediately spot Hugo's friends, but she did spot the man in question who, as always, beamed when he saw her. Autumn floated out of the way, as she tended to do when Jones was around Hugo. He walked from behind the bar, came over and kissed her. "Weird day, huh."

"Tell me about it," said Jones. "The smoke, the heat. And the Bank was so quiet today. How about you?"

Putting his arm around Jones, he nodded. "Very quiet for lunch. Things are getting a little busier now. Not sure how it will be this evening. Whether everyone will hunker down at home or feel like grabbing a drink."

"Well, I know I certainly need a drink!"

"I can sort that out," said Hugo. "But first come with me. As you know, there are some people I want you to meet."

Jones glanced up at Hugo, raising her eyebrows a little.

"They'll love you!" he said, reading her mind. "Come on."

Hugo led her to the beer garden outside, Autumn hovering off to one side. Jones was surprised anyone was sitting out here, what with the heat and the smokey air. There was a group of three men sitting around a table that was positioned in one of the few shady spots in the wine bar's garden. Each had a jacket of some sort flung on the back of their chairs, and three motorbike helmets were lined up against the wall. Two men leant their elbows on the table, sipping their bears, listening. The third man was leaning back, leg across his knee, looking up to the sky as he regaled his audience with a story. He was the last one to notice Jones as she walked over to them.

"You must be Jones!" A man with dusty red hair and a thick russet beard stood up, extending his hand as he walked towards her.

"Jones, this is Robert, also unsurprisingly known as Rusty."

"Call me Rusty! Not even my mum calls me Robert!" Jones shook the hand of this smiling man. She began to feel more at ease.

The storyteller had since leapt up, eager to be next in line. His head was closely shaven, and he too sported a beard, his longer and black. The sight of him caused Jones to freeze momentarily.

"Now this bloke looks a lot scarier than he is," said Hugo, once again proving himself an adept mind reader. "Jones, meet Chappy. Justin Chapman."

"Nice to meet you, Justin," said Jones. Feeling very unsure of herself. This man looked nothing like a Justin.

"You can call me Justin if you like," he said. "Just know I may mistake you for my wife. If you're ok with it, I'd be very happy for you to call me Chappy."

Jones smiled. This man wasn't scary at all. "Well then, nice to meet you, Chappy."

"There we go!" and he pulled her into a bear hug which Jones accepted awkwardly.

"Finally," said Hugo. "This here is Phoenix."

This man appeared younger than the others, although that could have been because he was clean-shaven, and had a full head of light brown hair that was messily swept back away from his face. He looked as nervous as Jones felt. He just glanced at her and nodded.

Jones offered him a slight smile. "Hi, Phoenix. Or do you have another name too?"

That did bring a smile to his face and he shook his head, but still didn't utter a word.

"That's what you get for being born the year Stand By Me came out," said Hugo. "I think his mum chose between River and Phoenix, and Phoenix won!"

"Oh, I loved that movie!" said Jones.

"Come on Jones, pull up a chair," said Chappy, bringing a seat over to their table. "Hugo, grab your girl a drink. She looks parched!"

Hugo winked at Jones and made his way back into the bar. Jones took her seat and twisted her fingers in her lap. She knew next to nothing about these guys, so had no idea how to start a conversation with them.

"A bit hot for motorbike riding today, I would have thought?"

"That's why Chappy had us up early," said Rusty. "Don't think I've been up before five in years."

"What did ya get up that early for?" Chappy said, finishing the beer in front of him.

"I didn't want to be late," said Rusty. "I know what you're like! I'd never hear the end of it."

"True that," said Chappy, turning to Jones. "Rusty here is known for being ambiguous with the time."

Jones laughed at his phrasing. She had a feeling she was going to like Chappy.

"Well, Chappy had us all meeting at Verdun at nine o'clock," said Rusty. "Still had to wait on Phoenix anyway. We've come from all directions. No idea why we couldn't all just meet here."

Jones had a pretty good idea. She glanced at Chappy. He wanted to make an entrance.

"Have you guys been to Lilly Pilly Creek before?" she asked.

Jones glanced at the three of them, trying to catch Phoenix's eye, but he had his head down, staring at something in his hands.

"Barely even heard of the place before Hugo told us about it," said Rusty. "'I'm starting a wine bar' he told us!"

"'A what?' we said." Chappy laughed. "We always knew Hugo was a bit posh, but a wine bar? Then when he told us where he was starting it. God, we thought he'd gone mad!"

Rusty and Chappy laughed, and Jones even noticed a grin from Phoenix.

"Here we are!" Hugo returned, holding a tray of beers and a sparkling rosè for Jones. He handed Jones her glass, but let the three men fetch their pints.

"I don't see enough beers on here!" said Chappy. "Aren't you taking the night off?"

"I'll be out shortly," said Hugo. "There's just been a bit of a run-on. Seems a bunch of the CFS blokes have knocked off, so they're heading in for some well-deserved drinks."

"Does that mean the fire's out?" asked Jones.

"Not out I don't think," said Hugo. "But they don't need the whole lot of them out there anymore."

"Atlas?" Jones looked up at Hugo, biting her lip.

He shook his head, not taking his eyes off her. "I haven't seen him yet. I'll send him out as soon as he comes in." Hugo walked back into the bar.

"Who's Atlas?" Rusty asked.

Jones spent the next few minutes explaining who Atlas was, which led her to explain what exactly The Memory Bank was, why she was there, and of course, what happened to her sister.

"Bloody hell!" said Chappy. Even Phoenix had raised his head whilst Jones was telling her story.

"Bloody hell, indeed," said Jones. "But I supposed there's always a silver lining. I've met Hugo." Jones felt her cheeks redden, and she looked at the ground. She hadn't meant to get quite so soppy around these men.

"Absolutely!" boomed Chappy. "And you've scored a good one there Jones. They don't come any better than Hugo."

Jones looked up at him and smiled. All three looked at her happily. They clearly had a strong bond and thought very highly of Hugo.

"I reckon Hugo's done alright too," said Rusty, raising his glass towards Jones. Her cheeks went even pinker and she laughed before gulping her wine.

"Here, here!" called out Autumn, a cheeky grin on her face from her position hovering behind the group.

"Alright," said Hugo. "What have they been telling you?" He'd returned with more beers and a wine, which he placed on the table before swinging a chair around to join them.

"Don't tell him, Jones!" Chappy said in mock seriousness.

Jones laughed and patted Hugo's knee. "To be honest I've been yabbering on a bit long, and haven't even asked about you guys. How did you all meet?"

The group went silent, picking up their beers and sipping, all eyes on Hugo. They were handballing this question to him. Jones caught Autumn's eye, who raised her eyebrows.

"Ah, well, the thing is," Hugo looked at Jones, then back at Chappy who was nodding. Jones felt her chest tighten. What on earth was he going to reveal? Had they met in prison? Were they a bikie gang? Were they fugitives on the run?

Hugo took her hand, indicating that he wanted her to look at him. Jones gulped and then looked into Hugo's eyes. What was happening?

"The thing is, Jones," said Hugo. Jones nodded at him, attempting to appear encouraging but still unable to take a breath. "So, we ah-"

"Jones," a voice called. Her head shot up. It was Atlas.

CHAPTER 6

"Oh, Atlas!" Jones rose quickly and stood in front of him. "Are you ok? How did you go?"

Autumn had whizzed over and was floating at Jones's side.

"I'm fine, I'm fine," he said, a grin on his face. "It was crazy! But I'm ok. Everyone's so professional. They had it under control fairly quickly."

"Oh, that's good."

"A local lad driving past with his Pop spotted the smoke. If we hadn't gotten out there so quickly Rhys Bauer's shed would have gone up."

Jones could tell Atlas had enjoyed his first fire.

"So, you weren't scared at all?" asked Jones. She was almost put out by his apparent joy when she had been worrying all day. "Have you called your mum?"

"Well, I guess there were a couple of scary moments," said Atlas. "But I just had to get out of the way and let the more experienced people deal with it. And yes, I've spoken to Mum. I went home and had a shower before I got here."

"Of course, of course," said Jones. She couldn't help herself. She grabbed him and pulled him into a hug. "I'm just glad you're ok."

"Honestly," said Autumn, shaking her head but grinning.

"I'm fine Jones," said Atlas. "Have you been worrying all day?"

"Not all day," said Jones, tilting her head and smiling.

"You're just like my mum!" said Atlas with a laugh. "Jones, I wondered, could I speak to you for a moment." He jabbed his head to the side, indicating he wanted some privacy. That didn't include Autumn who glided after Jones as she and Atlas moved to a quiet corner of the garden.

"What is it Atlas?" asked Jones, frowning, now worried all the bravado had just been for a show in front of Hugo's friends.

"I thought you'd be interested in hearing how the fire started," said Atlas, folding his arms across his chest.

"Absolutely I would!"

Atlas grinned at that and then leaned in, whispering. "Arson."

"No!" cried Jones before clamping her hand over her mouth.

"Yeah, not many people know, so we'd better be quiet," said Atlas. "I just happened to overhear the Captain on the phone. I think she was speaking to the police. Probably even Christopher. She very clearly said that it looks like arson."

"I can't believe it," said Jones. "Who would do such a thing!"

"I suppose it happens more than we realise," said Atlas. "But the way I saw all those women and men put their lives on the line out there today. Honestly, I'm livid."

"I bet you are! Did you tell your mum and dad this?"

Atlas shook his head. "No, I didn't want to worry them. I guess the word will come out soon enough."

"Yes, the rumour mill will start spinning."

"So, what do you reckon? Are you going to investigate?"

"What?" Jones spluttered. She could hear Autumn laughing next to her.

"You know," said Atlas. "Do your thing. Find the culprit."

"My thing?"

"You can't deny it, Jones," said Atlas. "Without you, numerous crimes in Lilly Pilly Creek would still be unsolved."

"Don't be ridiculous," said Jones. "They would have worked it out eventually."

Atlas raised his eyebrows. "Really?"

"Really," said Jones. "Now, I think I should be buying you a drink."

She pushed passed Atlas and made her way into the bar. As Hugo had predicted, members of the CFS were milling around inside, drinking beers or spirits, and discussing the day's events.

"What do you want?" Jones asked Atlas, as they stood at the bar. The two staff behind the counter were rather run off their feet.

"A beer is fine," said Atlas. "A pale ale. But I can pay for it."

"Don't be silly!" said Jones. "Of course, I'm buying you a beer. You just put out your first fire!"

"Helped," said Atlas. "I helped put out my first fire."

"Whatever you say," said Jones, turning to look at him. "But you do realise, there are so many people in the Hills, but only a select few put their hand up to fight these fires. You should be very proud of yourself."

Atlas looked down but nodded and smiled.

"What can I get you?" asked the woman behind the bar.

Once Jones had paid and Atlas had his beer, she turned around and looked across the bar. It had certainly filled since she'd first arrived, and more people were braving the outside area as the main bar filled.

She spotted one familiar face at a small table inside. Wren. And she was sitting with the woman from the Christmas party.

"The mysterious girlfriend," whispered Autumn.

"Atlas, I'm just going to say hi to Wren," said Jones.

"No worries," said Atlas. "Thanks for the beer!" He raised his glass before moving over to a group of men and women standing at the other end of the bar.

"Wren! Why hello!" Jones spoke rather cheekily. She had yet to formally meet the woman opposite Wren, the woman who had seemingly captured her best friend's heart, when no one else so far had succeeded, despite many attempts.

Wren lifted her head and then smiled at the sight of her friend. "Hi, Jones."

"Hi Wren," said Jones, and then turning dramatically to the woman opposite Wren. "Hi, I'm Jones," she said, putting her hand out.

"I know her," said Autumn. But before Autumn could say any more, the woman smiled back at Jones, took her hand and introduced herself.

"Hi Jones," she said. "I'm Mirri. I've heard a lot about you."

"Mirri! From High School," said Autumn. "Wow, I haven't seen her in years."

"Have you now," Jones responded, wiggling her way onto the bench seat next to Wren. "Well, I'm looking forward to hearing more about you. Wren is rather good at keeping secrets."

Jones glanced at her friend who was rolling her eyes. But Mirri didn't take offence. "You're right about that," said Mirri. "But granted, I have been with my family in the South East for the summer holidays."

"Mirri is a teacher," Wren explained. "Actually, she's starting at Lilly Pilly Creek Primary School this year."

"Oh really!" said Jones, leaning forward, resting her chin on her hand.

"Yes," said Mirri. "I've been at Lenswood Primary School the last few years, but will be teaching year three fours at Lilly Pilly Creek."

"That will be a change," said Jones. Lenswood Primary School was rather small in comparison to Lilly Pilly Creek. Not that it was a huge school, but it was much bigger than Lenswood. "So, are you from around here?"

"I am," said Mirri. "Kind of. Echunga. But I think I went to school with your sister. Autumn, right?"

"Did you go to Cornerstone College too?"

"Yes," said Mirri. "We used to hang out a lot when we were in year eleven and twelve, but then we lost touch."

"I would have been at University then," said Jones. "I don't think we ever met?"

Mirri shook her head. "Not that I can recall. I was so sorry to hear about her death. A few of us came to the funeral. From school. But there were so many people there."

Jones smiled and nodded, remembering Autumn's funeral. It was one of the biggest Lilly Pilly Creek had ever seen.

"Ah, now you can meet Hugo too," said Wren, looking over Jones's shoulder. Jones turned to see Hugo walking up to the group.

"How are we ladies?" he asked, flashing his broad smile.

"Hugo, I don't think you've met Mirri?" said Wren.

Hugo extended his hand. "Lovely to meet you, *finally*, Mirri." The group laughed and Hugo turned to Jones.

"There's someone at the bar looking for you," he said, indicating a woman, perched on a stool, a large camera hanging around her neck.

Jones squinted, trying to work out who it was. At that moment, the woman turned in her direction, smiled, and started waving frantically.

Jones had no idea who she was.

CHAPTER 7

"Jones!" The woman leapt off her stool and pushed her way through the crowd towards her. "Jones! There you are!"

"Who on earth is that?" asked Autumn.

Jones was horrified. Who indeed? She watched as the woman with her high blonde ponytail got closer. She was quite short and would occasionally get lost behind the taller patrons, before popping up again. She was wearing a navy polo t-shirt, olive shorts, and hiking boots.

Fortunately, as the woman bounced up to them, Jones finally worked out who it was.

"Quinn!" Jones exclaimed. "What are you doing here?"

"Thank goodness I found you," said Quinn, beaming at her. "I've been reporting on the fire."

Jones slapped her forehead. Of course, she was. Quinn McCoy was a colleague from The Advertiser newspaper, where Jones had worked up until a few months ago. Jones was currently on unpaid leave, so technically she was still employed by them, although if she were honest, it didn't feel like it. Quinn wasn't someone she knew particularly well. She was a newer journalist, still finding her feet, at least that was the impression Jones had previously. Being out solo on a bushfire job might mean she'd moved up the ranks a little.

"Did you get close?" Jones asked, lasering in on what was important to a reporter. "Who did you speak to?"

"I've done well, I think," she said, looking earnestly at Jones. "I've got quotes from the Captain, the local Sergeant, and I'm working on getting something from the Chief Officer, but the promo team keep blocking me."

Jones nodded in understanding. "I can imagine."

"Anyway," said Quinn, scrunching her nose. "I wondered if I could ask a favour?"

"Sure, what do you need?" said Jones. She was more than happy to share her words of wisdom with a keen reporter.

"A place to stay," said Quinn.

Jones stammered but quickly covered it by coughing. "Oh, ah, well, I don't know what's available around here. You might have to look it up online."

Quinn shook her head. "I have, and being January school holidays, everything is completely booked out. The closest place I can find is back in Adelaide, so I may as well just go home. But I'd rather not have to travel back and forth."

"So you think you'll need to be here tomorrow?"

"Absolutely," the woman responded. "I'm pitching a bit of a feature, so want to pull things together, on the ground."

"A feature hey," said Jones. "Sounds good."

"It does, I know," said Quinn, nodding.

"Confident much," said Autumn.

Jones took a deep breath, doing her best to remain unimpacted by Autumn's comments, despite the fact she was saying exactly what Jones was thinking.

"Anyway," she continued. "I was hoping I might be able to stay with you?"

"With me?" Jones was surprised. She barely knew this girl, and instead of just taking the forty-or-so-minute drive back to Adelaide, she was asking to stay at Jones's house. "Oh, ah, well, I suppose so. I'd have to make up a bed for you." Her mind was whirring as she tried to work out where she could put this girl. Not Autumn's room, no way. She supposed she'd have to offer her their parent's room, although the thought made her feel a little uncomfortable.

"That's fine," said Quinn. "Put me anywhere. On the couch even. I'm not fussy!"

"Ok, well, I'm not going home for a little while. I'm having tea with friends," she told Quinn. "What were your plans?"

"No problems. I was going to grab a quick bite myself. Then I thought I might head back out and see if I can get some sunset shots. You know how good those can be." Quinn nodded at Jones. Jones wasn't sure if she was trying to flatter Jones or elevate herself to Jones's level. Either way, Jones didn't bother to tell Quinn that she usually had a camera person with her to take those shots, and she'd normally be back writing the story whilst the camera person worked their magic. Tonight though, that was entirely beside the point. She not only had to go back out to eat with Hugo's friends, but she now had to look after an unexpected house guest.

Jones gave Quinn directions to her house, and a spare key just in case she needed it, and then watched the woman wind her way back to the bar to order her meal.

"I don't think I've ever used the word perky," said Autumn. "But, I think she's the walking definition."

"A bouncing definition, don't you mean," said Jones under her breath as she made her way out into the beer garden. Autumn chortled loudly, and Jones shook her head with a smile.

Hugo stood as Jones arrived at the table, and pulled a chair out for her. It was a little formal, but Jones couldn't deny she enjoyed it.

"I've just put a bit of everything on the table," he explained.

"I can see that," Jones said, eyeing off the platters of food before them. She glanced up. Three men were staring at her. It took a moment for Jones to understand what was going on. "Eat! You don't have to wait for me."

There was a lot of chivalry going on at this table but that quickly evaporated. Hugo's friends loaded their plates with hot chips, salt and pepper squid, pita bread, mini burgers, grilled halloumi and even a bit of peach, feta and rocket salad. Once they were done, Hugo indicated for Jones to serve her plate.

They all ate in silence for a moment. Jones knew their previous conversation had been interrupted. The conversation where Hugo appeared to be about to reveal something important. Yet Jones had a nagging feeling he wasn't ready to tell her about him and his friends. Wasn't quite ready to share it with Jones. So, she didn't push it. Didn't bring it up again.

Perhaps more pressing was the fact that Atlas had revealed to her that today's fire was arson, and, for some reason, his first inclination was to suggest that Jones investigate the case. It was ridiculous of course. There were experts no doubt already on the case. There was nothing she could offer to the investigation. Just because she had some luck, and a ghost, on her side in the past, didn't mean she was an investigator. Although if Autumn could read her mind, which thankfully she could not, she imagined her sister would be very enthusiastic about a new 'case' for the Eldershaw Sisters Detective Agency.

Jones smiled as she glanced up. Chappy was adding more food to his plate. Rusty was wiping up his with a piece of sourdough, and Phoenix who had finished, was once again staring down at his hands. Jones looked to her right at Hugo. He met her eyes, smiled, and squeezed her knee. It was comfortable. She hadn't expected to feel comfortable with Hugo's friends. Certainly not at this early stage. But for some reason, she felt more at home with this group of burly men than she had felt in a long time. She realised that whatever Hugo had been about to tell her, it couldn't be that bad. Could it?

Looking up at Autumn, Jones smiled, before quickly frowning. Autumn was pointing at Phoenix.

"Look what he's got in his hand!"

CHAPTER 8

Jones had to ignore Autumn until the end of dinner. She locked eyes with her sister, subtly shook her head, and turned to talk with Hugo's friends. She had no idea what Autumn was referring to, but whatever it was, she didn't want it to disrupt the pleasant meal they were sharing. Autumn had attempted to protest, but Jones had ignored her, so she floated over to the banks of Lilly Pilly Creek and left Jones to it.

"So, you're staying at Hugo's?" Jones asked. "Where will you all sleep?" Jones had only been to Hugo's house once. If you could call it a house. It was a one-bedroom tiny house with very minimal facilities. Yet it was set on a gorgeous block of land, surrounded only by trees and a stunning view out over the Lobethal Range.

"We've got our swags!" piped up Rusty.

"Of course you do," Jones laughed.

She recalled the bikes lined up at the front of Hugo's. Each one had a rolled-up canvas tied to the back. The swag, a type of bed roll, dated back to the early days of Australia when men, and some women, travelled Australia in search of work. They'd carry their swag over their shoulder, along with a billy to boil water, tools of their trade, and anything else they needed to survive on the road. Nowadays the swag is still a very popular item, particularly with young men and women from the country, heading off camping or going to off-the-grid events like country rodeos or BnS Balls, originally called Bachelor and Spinster's Balls. Any excuse to have a giant party in the middle of a paddock.

"We've roughed it a lot worse than that," said Chappy, taking a final gulp of beer. "And with that, I think we'd better shoot off before it gets too dark."

The men stood up from the table, Rusty also quickly finishing his pint.

Hugo turned to Jones. "I'd better show them the way," he said, before leaning in to give her a peck on the cheek. "See you tomorrow?"

Jones smiled. "See you tomorrow." Then turning to the three friends. "Have fun!"

Jones watched the four of them walk into the bar and then out the front doors. Autumn had returned to Jones's side and they began a whispered conversation.

"Funny bunch," she said.

"Oh, they seemed nice enough, don't you think?"

Autumn shrugged. "I'm not sure. Rusty and the other guy, what was his name?"

"Chappy."

"Yeah him. They seemed nice. But there's something off about Phoenix."

"He's just quiet," said Jones.

The sisters stood watching the crowd. The evening hadn't cooled much but some groups were mingling outside, trying to catch a whisper of a breeze. The firefighters seemed to have dispersed. Either home to bed after an exhausting day or relieving their crew mates who would still be monitoring the smouldering ashes.

"Did you see what he had in his hand all night?"

"What? A beer?" Jones said this with noticeable sarcasm.

"Ha ha," said Autumn. "No. Not the beer. I'll give you a hint. Atlas."

"He was holding an atlas?" said Jones. "He was holding Atlas?" She turned to Autumn scrunching her eyebrows, very confused.

"No, think. What did Atlas tell you?"

"About the fire? The arson?"

"Yes," said Autumn.

"And that has something to do with what Phoenix was holding? Was he holding fire?"

"Yes!" Autumn flew to face Jones. "Exactly. He was holding fire. A cigarette lighter to be precise."

"He was?" Jones's mouth gaped a little.

"He was," said Autumn. "He'd flick the button, stare at the flame, lift his finger, and then do it all again. Over and over again."

"How could I not have noticed that?" Jones glanced back at the table where they'd all been sitting. "But you don't think?"

Autumn tilted her head. "What, that he could have a penchant for lighting fires?"

"You can't go accusing someone you've only just met of, of...." Jones stammered. She couldn't say it.

"Arson?" said Autumn. "Well, no, I suppose I shouldn't go around accusing random people. But you have to admit it's a little suspicious considering the day we've had."

Jones sighed. "Well, I'm not saying anything. Especially to Hugo.

Can you imagine? I finally meet his friends for the first time, and I accuse one of them of arson."

"Probably not a great start," Autumn agreed.

"Right, well I'd better get home and set up a bed for my surprise visitor," said Jones. She made her way through the bar, said a quick goodbye to Wren and Mirri, noted Atlas had already left, and continued out onto the footpath.

"Was that her name? Quinn?" Autumn asked as they walked to The Memory Bank. "A bit cheeky don't you reckon? Inviting herself to stay."

"Quite presumptuous," said Jones. "I mean I hardly know her. It's like she had it all worked out in her head, and only asked me as a courtesy!"

"I suppose you'll barely see her," said Autumn. "Are you going to give her the scoop?"

"What? About the fire being arson?" Jones made her way over to her Mini.

Autumn nodded but Jones shook her head. "No, I can't do that. I couldn't betray Atlas like that. Plus it's not official. I'll let her go through the right channels."

"Did you always go through the right channels?" Autumn raised her eyebrows.

"Well of course not," said Jones. "But this is different."

"Different how?"

"Well, I just think she needs to work it out for herself," said Jones.

"Ah, you're teaching her a lesson," said Autumn, a smirk on her face.

"Exactly!" Jones grinned unlocking her car and opening the driver's door. "Alright, I'll leave you here. See you in the morning."

"See you in the morning!" Autumn's voice rang out as she slid through the stone wall of The Memory Bank.

It didn't take long for Jones to make her way home. The sun was setting as she pulled into the driveway, causing the cream stone of the old house to glow orange. Stepping out of her car, she turned to take in the sight of the brilliant glow, disappearing behind the Mount Lofty Ranges. It was a stunning sunset, but she couldn't help but compare the firey colour of the sky to the flames that had burnt today, not all that far away.

The fact it was arson caused Jones to shiver, despite the warm evening. The idea that there was someone out there deliberately lighting fires was horrifying. The danger it put everyone in, and the obvious recklessness when it came to the property of others, not to mention the lives that could be lost. Was Autumn right? Was Phoenix responsible? She knew nothing about him, and she had to admit, he was a little quiet. But did that make him capable of lighting a bush fire? Jones didn't want to rush to judgment yet.

CHAPTER 9

Jones was up early, searching her cupboards for something she could offer Quinn for breakfast. In the end, she decided the effort was fruitless, and she left a note for Quinn saying she was dashing to Sybil's to pick up coffee and something to eat.

Today she had slipped on a tank top with the quote "We meet no ordinary people in our lives." by C.S. Lewis. Jones hoped she could use this as an affirmation to deal with some of the unexpected visitors who had appeared in her world over the past twenty-four hours. She hoped she could look at them with kindness and curiosity, rather than annoyance and judgement.

"Let's hope that fire's out," said Sybil once Jones had placed her order. An older couple with a greyhound were standing waiting for their order as the two women chatted.

"I know," said Jones. "Sounds like it was a bit scary. Not that Atlas would admit to that."

"Oh yes, Atlas at his first fire. How did he go?"

"He said everything was fine. That it was all handled professionally."

"As you would expect," said Sybil. "Even though they're volunteers, the CFS are very well trained and take things seriously. We're lucky to have them."

Jones nodded, then stood quietly as Sybil steamed milk for the dog owners's coffees. She wasn't sure if she should mention to Sybil what Atlas had told her. Jones wondered why she was holding back. She and Sybil often shared the town's secrets. But for some reason, this felt different. As though it wasn't her secret to share. Perhaps she would wait and see what Sybil had to say.

As soon as the couple had left, Sybil got right to preparing the flat whites, eggs benedict and bacon rolls, and some corn and potato fritters.

"I seem to have acquired a visitor," Jones said, to explain the larger-than-usual order.

"Oh yes, that journalist who's in town," replied Sybil.

"How did you know that?" said Jones, but then laughed. "Well, of course, you knew. What was I thinking?"

"Did you work together?"

"I knew of her I guess," said Jones. "We had seen each other around the office. I wouldn't say we were close though."

"So why is she staying with you?"

Jones laughed at Sybil's to-the-point observation. "I have no idea!"

"And updates on the arsonist?" Sybil asked, keeping her eyes on the milk she was steaming.

"So you *do* know about that," said Jones, a sigh of relief escaping her mouth. "But how did you know I knew?"

Sybil lifted her eyes to Jones and grinned. "I've got to have some secrets."

"Fair enough," said Jones. "Well, no I haven't heard anything since last night. I imagine they'll make it public soon enough?"

"Perhaps," said Sybil. "As long as it doesn't jeopardise the investigation."

Jones nodded. Sybil was right. Perhaps it wouldn't get media coverage in case it scared away the arsonist before they could catch them. This confirmed her decision not to tell Quinn. It could have much bigger consequences than just betraying Atlas's confidence.

Sybil handed Jones a bag full of the breakfast foods, and a tray to carry the coffees, and went straight to serving the the mum's with prams who had just arrived.

With one hand on the tray of coffees to ensure they didn't spill, Jones drove back home. As she unlocked the front door and entered, she heard footsteps coming from the back room.

"Let me help you with that!" The tiny whirlwind that was Quinn McCoy dashed down the hall, her high ponytail flipping behind her. Today she was wearing black shorts, a black singlet, and a short-sleeved unbuttoned shirt over the top.

"Loving your top!" Quinn said as she carried the coffee into the kitchen. "You're certainly not ordinary, Jones."

Jones turned her back to Quinn, grinning and raising her eyebrows. "Thank you, Quinn." She put the breakfast onto plates, and placing knives and forks on the side, brought them to the breakfast bar.

"This looks delicious!" said Quinn. "Thank you!"

"Some of Sybil's specialities. I love the eggs benedict roll."

"Eggs benedict roll?" said Quinn. "I've never had eggs benedict in a roll. That's genius."

Jones smiled, sipping her coffee. "Sybil is quite a genius."

The two ate in silence, Jones quickly making her way through her corn fitter, before taking the roll in two hands, allowing the egg yolk and Benedict sauce to run down her wrist.

"So, what are your plans for the day?" she asked Quinn.

With her mouth full, Quinn nodded, and smiled, chewing for a moment, before swallowing. "I'm going to the fire ground first. Want to get some shots. And hoping some of the big wigs might rock up so I can get an interview."

Jones nodded, not envying Quinn heading out to cover a fire. It was always tough contending with the heat and smoke, not to mention the sadness of seeing the aftermath.

"Has any property been destroyed?" Jones asked.

"Oh no, I don't think so!" said Quinn, her eyes wide.

Jones frowned a little, unsure why Quinn appeared shocked by this question. She supposed being her first fire story, she hadn't quite grasped the seriousness of the situation. Jones finished her roll in silence, realising Quinn may have an eye-opening day. It was the life of a journalist after all.

"How long have you been with The Advertiser now?" asked Jones.

"It's almost three years," said Quinn. "I can't believe it."

"And before The Advertiser? Where were you?"

"Oh, I worked for The Bunyip at Gawler. That's where I did my cadetship."

So Jones was right. Quinn was still a relatively new journalist. To get the fire story, and to be on the road by herself, she must have some talent.

"Are you still working with Jock?" Jones asked. Jock was one of the editors at The Advertiser. She'd worked with him a few years ago.

"Yes," said Quinn. "I'm not sure what he thinks of me. I can't read him."

Jones laughed at this. "That's Jock. Don't worry, I still can't read him."

Quinn sighed. "Thank goodness. I thought it was just me!"

"Nope," said Jones. "I think he likes to act aloof. Probably thinks it makes him seem like an editor for the New York Times or something."

The two women laughed together and finished their breakfast.

"Have the papers arrived yet?" Quinn asked. Jones frowned, not sure what she meant.

"Oh, you want to see your story from yesterday." It finally clicked. "Sorry, I hadn't bothered to get deliveries here. You'll have to visit the newsagent. I think they open at nine."

Quinn sighed. It was only just after eight. Jones understood. In the city, the newspaper often landed on your front step before six.

"Maybe grab another coffee while you wait?" she suggested. "Sometimes Margaret opens up a few minutes early."

"Another coffee sounds perfect," said Quinn.

"If you're ready now, I'll introduce you to Sybil on the way," said Jones. "I need another coffee too."

CHAPTER 10

"Sybil, I'd like to introduce you to a fellow journalist," said Jones. "This is Quinn McCoy."

"Lovely to meet you, Quinn," said Sybil, extending her arm. "What are you reporting on in Lilly Pilly Creek?"

"The fire," said Quinn. "I'm hoping to have a cover story today." Quinn smiled, and Jones held back her inclination to scoff. No wonder she was so desperate to get the paper. Jones looked down at her sandals, taking great pains to look at each painted toenail before lifting her head, having composed herself.

"Oh," said Sybil. "So you heard about-"

"Heard about how amazing the CFS is," said Jones. She cut Sybil off and did a slight shake of her head. Quinn didn't know about the arson, and until she heard it from official channels, Jones was hoping the murmurings wouldn't come Quinn's way.

"They are amazing," said Quinn. "I'd love to do a feature about everyone involved actually. I think it's a great story."

"Well, you'll need to speak with Candace Chadwick," said Sybil. "She's the Lilly Pilly Creek CFS Captain."

"Yes I believe I spoke with her yesterday," said Quinn. "Today I'm hoping to chat with the main guy, the Chief." She glanced at her watch. "I'd be there already if I had a newspaper."

Jones glanced at Quinn, not missing the obvious dig she'd made. "Breakfast was delicious Sybil," she said to change the subject.

"Oh yes," said Quinn. "How did you come up with an eggs

benedict roll?"

"I needed a way to make eggs benedict portable, so I just glammed up the classic egg and bacon roll," said Sybil, her eyes sparkling. Sybil loved it when people gushed over her food.

"Meanwhile, I am hoping the fire is contained," said Sybil. "That was close enough thank you very much."

Jones nodded. "I agree. Let's hope that's the only fire we have to be concerned about. That being said, if anyone needs somewhere cool to go if anything does happen, please feel free to let people know they are more than welcome to come to The Memory Bank."

Sybil nodded. "Thanks, Jones. I'll make sure to pass that on."

Quinn and Jones thanked Sybil for their second coffee of the day and made their way to the newsagent.

"Morning Margaret!" Jones waved at the older woman putting an A-Frame onto the footpath, encouraging people to stock up on back-to-school supplies.

"Hi Jones," said the woman. "Another hot one today."

Jones nodded, a slight frown on her face. "Here's hoping there's no fire bells today."

"Too right"

"Margaret, this is Quinn," introduced Jones. "She's a journalist from town, covering the fire."

Margaret smiled and turned to walk back into the news agency. "Lovely to meet you, Quinn. How can I help you?"

"I need a copy of The Advertiser. I presume today's edition has arrived?" Quinn and Jones followed Margaret into her store. In front of them was a display of colourful pencil cases and water bottles. The walls were lined with shelves full of stationery items, and in the middle were rows of magazines and gift cards, as well as wrapping paper and toys.

"Just up here by the counter," Margaret said, weaving her way through the store to the counter on one side. She grabbed a newspaper from the stack and handed it to Quinn. Quinn quickly laid it on the counter and began flicking through the pages.

"Where is it?" Quinn's brow was furrowed and she let out a huge groan. "Page five! Come on!"

Jones walked next to Quinn and peered at the page in front that was open. There was an article taking up a quarter of the page. *Adelaide Hills Bushfire Controlled.* A few paragraphs flowed underneath Quinn's byline. It was a well-written article, but Quinn was clearly disappointed.

"Page five is great, Quinn," said Jones. "When I first started I rarely got on page five."

"But I was sure it would be a bigger story! I was *told* it would be a big story." Quinn quickly flicked to the front page and almost growled. "Of course, a Royal Family story trumps me!" Quinn picked up the paper and angrily rolled it under her arm. She quickly paid Margaret with barely a nod of thanks and left the shop.

"Bye, Margaret!" Jones called as she rushed after Quinn.

"I'm sorry," said Jones, attempting to console Quinn. She understood how disappointing it was to have your article cut down when you've been told it would be one of the leads.

Quinn took a deep breath. "It's ok. I just have to do better today. I'm going to speak to the Chief if it kills me!"

"You've got this!" Jones called after Quinn, hoping she sounded encouraging. She stood for a moment, watching Quinn stride away.

"Oh, no!" Jones glanced at her watch. It was now a quarter past nine and she was fifteen minutes late opening The Memory Bank. Jones started jogging down the road, looking both ways before crossing at the pedestrian lights without waiting for them to change. With barely a glance at Hugo's, she rattled the key in the door, shoved it open and quickly pressed the alarm buttons.

"Where on earth have you been!" Jones was startled by the stern voice.

Autumn stood there, hands on her hips, her red hair in a tight bun, dressed like Anne of Green Gables in her teacher era. She appeared to be going for the stern headmistress look. She even had wire-rimmed glasses on.

"With Quinn of course," Jones said. "And what is this get up?"

"You like?" Autumn twirled. "I thought I needed to look the part if I was going to pull you in line for your tardiness."

Jones laughed. "Tardiness! Ha!"

"This dress is a bit uncomfortable though," she said, pulling at the puffy-sleeved jacket she wore. "At least, I imagine it would be if I could feel it." Autumn performed a quick twirl and she was now wearing a summer dress with spaghetti straps, her hair in a loose ponytail. "That's better!"

Jones shook her head, smiling. She was getting used to Autumn's dramatic outfit changes, but still couldn't help but be impressed.

"Anyway," said Autumn. "I've been dying to talk to you!

CHAPTER 11

"About Phoenix, I suppose?" said Jones, walking through the room.

"Oh yes, that too," said Autumn, swinging her legs over the counter as Jones got herself set up for the day.

"So there's something else?"

"Mirri! I can't believe Mirri is Wren's secret girlfriend."

"Oh yes," said Jones. "How lovely is she! Did you go to school with her?"

She walked to the front door and hung a sign on the outside that read "We are open and it's cool inside!" Jones kept the door of The Memory Bank closed on hot days, so she wanted to ensure no one was deterred from entering.

"Yes, we were best friends for two years," said Autumn. "We got each other through the end of school. Mirri was very studious. I don't think I would have done so well in year twelve without her."

"But surely I would have met her?" Jones said.

"You weren't around much back then," said Autumn.

"But I would have met Mirri when I came home if you were that close?"

"Don't you remember Jones?" asked Autumn, cocking her head to the side. "You barely ever came home. You'd escaped Lilly Pilly Creek."

"Escaped?" Jones frowned.

"All you used to talk about was getting out of the place," said

Autumn. "You and I were so different. You couldn't wait to leave."

Jones glanced at her sister. She saw her face was awash with sadness.

"I wasn't the best sister, was I?" Jones asked. Autumn raised her eyebrows but didn't say anything. Her silence said it all.

"Oh, Autumn," Jones reached out and walked towards Autumn, then abruptly stopped. She had instinctively gone to hug her sister. It was all she wanted to do. Yet, it was impossible. Immediately her eyes started to water. "Autumn, I'm so sorry. I know, I know, I was entirely focused on myself. I just left you and Dad in the dust."

Autumn shrugged. "Look, the past is the past. And now is probably not the time to have an emotional breakdown. You have a business to run!" Autumn smiled.

Jones nodded, tears dripping down her cheeks. She knew she had to talk about this more with her sister. She realised she hadn't taken much time to think about their relationship as sisters. Just assumed it was because they were so different. Of course, they didn't get on, especially when they were younger. But Autumn was forcing Jones to consider that maybe she, being the older sister, had something to do with it.

"I'll snap out of it," said Jones. "But I haven't forgotten. I promise we *will* have the conversation."

Autumn left Jones for a while to regroup, floating through the wall into her escape room.

Jones was moving around The Memory Bank, pulling down blinds in an attempt to keep the place as cool as possible. Fortunately, The

Memory Bank hadn't warmed up in the least, and Jones wanted to keep it that way.

She found a box of books that had been delivered the previous day and began restocking the shelves. Jones had been searching online for any books that were relevant to Lilly Pilly Creek and had found a secondhand seller online who stocked a lot of Australian history books and memoirs.

As she shelved, she replayed her conversation with Autumn that morning. It had brought to the surface a lot of insecurities Jones had suppressed for all these years. She had always convinced herself that she'd been a kind, caring and supportive sister and daughter. No, she hadn't returned to Lilly Pilly Creek often, but she'd always convinced herself her family understood. She was starting her career. Jones had always believed her father, and Autumn in particular, had their own lives and were happy for her to spread her wings.

Yet Autumn's comment had been jarring. Jones's desire to leave Lilly Pilly Creek had perhaps been too strong. She had expressed her need to leave often as she came to the end of high school, never once considering how that might feel to Autumn and their Dad. Jones realised being so adamant that Lilly Pilly Creek was not the place to be, meant she had unintentionally implied she didn't feel it was the right place for anyone. When of course, that wasn't true. But how was Autumn to know that? Clearly, she had hurt her younger sister, and Autumn had never forgotten it.

As she created a display of a selection of the books on a table near the entrance, Jones thought more about her family and their legacy.

Was there a way for her to make amends, no matter how belated? Being back in Lilly Pilly Creek, in The Memory Bank, with no one left except Autumn, she realised it was entirely up to her to carry on the family story and memories. Would a book be one way she could do that? Could it be a project she and Autumn could work on together? The idea began to lift her mood and she felt a flutter of excitement.

"How was it having a houseguest?"

Jones jumped, not noticing Autumn had reappeared.

"It was fine," said Jones, shaking her head a little to get over the fright. "Nice to chat with a journalist again. She was pleasant enough really."

"Well, it was only one night," said Autumn.

Jones glanced up at Autumn and then quickly lowered her eyes.

"You invited her to stay again?" Autumn's mouth was gaping.

"Well, not technically." Jones did her best to justify herself. "I didn't say she could stay tonight. I just said 'Anytime!' It's just one of those things you say. Right?"

"She doesn't seem like the type of person who is aware of boundaries," said Autumn, who, for some reason, was currently doing the worm past the chandelier.

"Probably not," said Jones. "I didn't get a chance to check her plans. She was too annoyed about her story getting on page five."

"Page five? That's not too bad, is it?"

"Not at all! Especially for a relatively new journalist like herself," said Jones. "But she is adamant she was promised a bigger story, so she's on a mission today."

"Heading back to the fire ground?' asked Autumn. "Well, then I'd say you should be expecting another house guest tonight.

"Oh no!" Jones cried out. And it wasn't because Quinn was likely going to be sleeping in her spare bed again that night. The sound of the fire bell was once again reverberating through the Bank.

"I'll see if I can spot smoke," Autumn shouted before twirling up and away through the ceiling.

Jones pulled out her phone and frantically tapped the CFS website. She scanned the incidents but nothing on the list appeared close as yet. Jones dashed to the counter, then to the garden door, and then back. She didn't know what to do. Jones honestly thought yesterday's bushfire was all they'd experience. A close call, but nothing to worry about. As the bell rang and rang, Jones realised she had not been anticipating she would need to be on alert again. And after the somewhat jolting conversation with Autumn, she was feeling decidedly unsteady.

"I can't see anything," said Autumn, diving back into the room. "Hopefully it means it's too far away for us to worry."

"Or just too soon to tell," said Jones.

"Well, that would be a good thing, right?" said Autumn. "Wouldn't that mean the alarm has been sounded early enough for them to get it under control?"

"I hope so," said Jones. She made her way to the counter, sat on a stool and rested her chin in her hands. All she could do was wait.

Jones heard the handle of the main door rattle.

"I bet it's Wren," said Autumn. "I saw her lugging a suitcase in this direction."

"Jones!" It *was* Wren and she was wheeling a small suitcase behind her. "Gosh, it's boiling out there!"

"It's awful," said Jones. "And it's barely ten o'clock!"

"Well, to make matters worse," said Wren. "The aircon in my office has just given up the ghost!"

"Oh no!" said Jones, ignoring Autumn's chuckle.

"Sybil gave me the hot tip that The Memory Bank was open to visitors," said Wren with a grin.

"Did she now," Jones replied cheekily. "That was in bush fire emergencies only."

"Can't you hear the bell?" Wren laughed and then sighed as the bell finally stopped. "Oh thank goodness. That was beginning to get annoying. For some reason, it's not quite as loud in my office and I'm right next to the fire station."

"I wonder if that means the fire is under control?"

"Here's hoping," said Wren. She leant her suitcase against the counter. "You don't mind if I work in here for a while do you?"

"Of course not," said Jones. "But why not just go home?" Wren lived in Lobethal which wasn't that far from Lilly Pilly Creek.

"Well, I had organised to have lunch with Mirri at Hugo's," said Wren, shrugging.

"Oh yes," said Jones. " The girlfriend who is flesh and blood!"

"Did you doubt me?"

Jones raised her eyebrows. "I *was* beginning to wonder why you we'd never met her. A lot of reasons were swirling around in my head."

"Tell her we love the new girlfriend," said Autumn, who unbeknownst to Wren, was standing at the counter right next to her.

"Well, she's lovely," said Jones. "And you most certainly can't miss a lunch with her. I can put you in one of the lockbox rooms if you like." Jones indicated the glass offices at the back of the Bank where people could securely add to their lockboxes.

"Perfect!"

Jones led the way and Wren followed, her suitcase wheels gently bumbling over the original timber floors.

When Wren was set up in her temporary office, all cool and collected, Autumn glided up to Jones to provide an update. "I didn't want to say anything whilst Wren was here, but the fire appears to be coming from Lobethal Range."

"What, near Hugo's?" Jones's eyes were wide.

"Yes, but from what I can see, it is blowing the other way," said Autumn. "And that means-"

"Towards Lobethal. Toward's Wren's house."

CHAPTER 12

"Look, let's just keep an eye on the alerts, and if there is anything concerning, then we'll tell her." Jones and Autumn were whispering between the bookshelves which contained local histories, memoirs, and other books enjoyed by their customers.

"Yes good idea," said Jones, pulling up her phone to check. "Nothing as yet."

"I suppose Atlas is out there again?" said Autumn.

"I would imagine so," said Jones. "The CFS guys must get exhausted."

"I wonder how close Quinn is managing to wangle herself," Autumn laughed and Jones couldn't help smiling, picturing the tiny figure of Quinn slipping around CFS trucks to get the best vantage point.

"As long as she keeps herself safe," said Jones. "But honestly, good for her. You do need to do the hard yards if you want to land a story."

"And it appears only the front page will do for her!" said Autumn. "Jones, how many front pages have you had in your time?"

"No idea," said Jones, bending down to look at a book on the bottom shelf.

"Yes, you do!" Autumn challenged her.

"I'm keeping that to myself," said Jones. Fortunately, she was saved by the sound of the Bank door opening.

Jones strode out into the room expecting to greet a customer. Instead, it was the local police Sergeant, Christopher Schmidt.

"Morning Christopher," said Jones. "Is everything alright?"

Christopher nodded and then quickly glanced around the room. "Is anyone else here?"

Jones almost mistakenly said Autumn but regained her composure. "Wren is working in one of the offices. Her air-conditioning isn't working. But other than that, no one else has been in at all."

"Can we talk," he said. "Privately?"

"Ooooh, privately," Autumn teased.

"Sure," said Jones. "We can sit over here. Wren's door is closed, and we'll notice if anyone else comes in."

Christopher and Jones sat down at one of the customer tables. The policeman was acting very formal. When it came to Christopher, Jones never quite knew what mode she was going to get. The kind and friendly man she knew him to be, or the serious and professional policeman.

"So, what's up?" Jones asked.

"I imagine you've already heard?"

Jones realised she knew exactly what he was talking about. She just wasn't sure why he would be coming to her about it and why he would presume to know she already had that sensitive piece of information. "About the cause of yesterday's fire?"

Christopher nodded. "Arson."

Jones sighed. "Awful."

"It is," said Christopher. "Do you mind me asking how you heard? Was it Sybil?"

"No," said Jones. "It was Atlas."

"It was?" Christopher raised his eyebrows. "That's interesting." He looked off into the distance.

"It is? How so?"

Christopher turned slowly back to her, clasped his hands in front of himself, and took a deep breath.

"The sad thing about arson is, often, not always, but often, the culprit is someone who," he paused and sighed. "Fights fires."

Jone's felt her stomach clench. "Yes, I have heard that before." She didn't dare say anything more.

"Well, I spoke with Candace, the local captain. Obviously, it's still early days."

Jones nodded, holding her breath.

"Look, I just have to come out and say it," he said. "But, you have to know this is completely unorthodox. I should not be having this discussion with you. At all. I just think I owe you, owe them…."

"I understand," said Jones. "I won't say anything to anyone." Fortunately, Jones and Christoper had been through enough that he could trust her word.

"Ok," he said. "Candace didn't want to point fingers, but I have to listen to her insight. She said that she trusts every single person on her crew, they would all risk their lives for each other."

"The CFS is amazing," Jones nodded, her hands gripping her thighs.

"The thing is, there is only one new volunteer on the crew."

Jones shook her but couldn't say a word. Couldn't say the name out loud.

"He can't possibly mean-" Autumn blurted. "No! No way!"

"Unfortunately, we have to consider all leads. This means that today," Christopher paused. "I need to interview Atlas."

Jones inhaled before letting out a long, loud breath. Many, many words were on the tip of her tongue, most of them Christopher would be shocked to hear come out of her mouth. She just managed to hold them in.

Autumn on the other hand had no qualms, spiralling around the room shouting to the only person who could hear her. Jones pushed herself out of the chair and started pacing the room as Autumn loudly expressed her point of view. Once her sister was done and she was feeling calmer she walked over to Christopher.

"We both know there is no way he possibly did this," she said. "Absolutely not. What do you need me to do?"

Christopher stood up. "Nothing at this stage. Just support Atlas. I'm going to have to question him at the police station, take a statement, and that can be very confronting."

"He needs a lawyer," said Jones. "He needs Wren."

"That is his choice," said Christopher. "But you can't give him the heads up. You can't say anything to him until I've contacted him."

"But, surely-"

"No Jones, you can't say a word."

"Ok, ok, I understand," said Jones. "But can you please, please make it clear to him that it is highly recommended he ring a lawyer and give him the chance to do that? Please?"

Christopher nodded. "I will do my best."

"Oh my goodness," said Jones. "Atlas will be devastated. Please be kind, Christopher. Please look after him." Jones looked up at Christopher, pleading with him.

He reached out and gripped her upper arm. "I'll do everything I can Jones."

Jones pressed her fingers to her forehead, rubbing. It was too much. "Thanks, Christopher. Thanks for letting me know. Are you going to see him now?"

"I'm heading out to this morning's fire," Christopher said. "I imagine he will be there."

"You don't think this one could be arson too?" The thought had only just occurred to Jones.

"I hope not," said Christopher, and he turned and left.

"You've got to be kidding me," said Autumn, zooming up to Jones. "There is no way Atlas is an arsonist!"

"Of course not," said Jones. "But just because he isn't, doesn't mean others can't accuse him."

"I bet it's her!" said Autumn.

"Who?"

"This Candace woman," said Autumn.

Jones glanced up and saw Wren looking at her. "Shhh," she said to Autumn under her breath. Jones smiled at Wren and then made as though to go and adjust some of the gift tables. It didn't take long for Wren to make an appearance.

"So, what did Christopher want?" Wren wandered over, arms

behind her back.

"I can't say anything Wren," said Jones. "You know how it is."

Wren smiled. "Yep, it's just usually me who can't say anything."

"Look, all I can tell you is that you'll probably know everything soon enough."

"Will I now?" Wren tilted her head to the side.

"Please don't do your lawyer thing on me," said Jones. "I promise, you will know everything soon."

"I'm just wondering what Sergeant Schmidt would have to speak to you about confidentially?" Wren continued. "Usually I'd be inclined to zero in on something personal. But the way you solve crimes in Lilly Pilly Creek, I wouldn't be surprised if you're getting some inside information."

"Oh, has she got you pegged!" Autumn laughed.

Jones shook her head. "Wren, that's enough. I'm not saying a thing. Don't you have work to do?"

"Yes," said Wren. "I have a walking meeting. It starts at Sybil's."

"A walking meeting?"

"Yep! Keep fit and work at the same time."

"And you can plan a legal defence that way?" Jones walked over to another table that really did need some rearranging.

Wren laughed. "You watch too much TV!"

Jones desperately wanted to tell Wren that she very well may need to 'mount a defence' quite soon, but instead did her best to appear nonchalant.

"Well, enjoy! At least you get to have one of Sybil's coffees whilst you walk. But isn't it a bit hot out there? And maybe smoky?"

Wren glanced at her watch. "Yes, it probably has started to heat up. We may just end up under a tree in the park. I'll see you when I get back!"

"Thank goodness she's gone," said Autumn as soon as the door closed.

"That's a bit rude," said Jones.

"You know what I mean!" her sister twirled in front of her. "We have so much to talk about. Can you believe Christopher!"

"I think you mean Candace. What's her name again? Candace Chiswick? Chadwack? Chad-WICK! How dare she accuse Atlas!" Jones strode around the bank, flinging her arms in the air, exasperated.

"It seems pretty obvious to me what's happening here," said Autumn, spinning to reveal her detective outfit, consisting of a red trench coat and a deer stalker hat.

"It does?"

"Candace is the arsonist and she's trying to pin it on Atlas."

Jones stopped in her tracks. "Oh my gosh! You could be right!"

Autumn shrugged at the obviousness of the comment. "Well, he did say that in these cases firefighters are usually the perpetrators."

"He didn't say that exactly," said Jones. "But it is a very interesting scenario."

"An obvious one in my mind," said Autumn. "I presume Christopher's clever enough to investigate her too."

"Of course he would be," said Jones. "You know how thorough he is."

"Yes, but how many cases has he solved of late? Independently?"

"You mean without the assistance of the Eldershaw Sisters Detective Agency?" Jones smirked a little.

"Exactly!"

"Are you saying what I think you're saying?"

CHAPTER 13

"Of course, we need to investigate!" Autumn was perched on a stool at the counter. She had procured herself a smoking pipe, which sat in her mouth, and she held a magnifying glass which she was pretending to peer through.

"Alright Sherlock," Jones said with a grin. "If I'm the Watson in this scenario, how do you propose we do that?"

"I have no idea."

Jones burst out laughing. "So what exactly am I supposed to do?"

"Again, I have no idea," pulling the pipe out of her mouth and pretending to puff smoke rings into the air.

Jones groaned and slumped down in a chair. "You're right, we do have to investigate. And we've been in this position before. We should be capable. We just have to think things through and work out what we can bring to the table. What are our key skill sets?"

"That's easy! Mine is eavesdropping," said Autumn. "And yours is manipulation."

"Manipulation?" Jones sat back in her seat, crossing her arms.

"In the best possible way!" Autumn whooshed over to sit in the chair opposite her sister. "Remember how you got Molly to talk, to confess. That's what I mean. You manipulated her. And she didn't even know you were doing it. You were brilliant!"

Jones allowed herself a small smile. Although she had no idea exactly how she'd done it, somehow she had managed to get Molly to confess to killing Lorne Fox, as well as participating in the theft of their own family's jewels. All in front of Sergeant Schmidt who was recording the whole thing. It *was* pretty clever.

"You do have a point," said Jones. "But neither of those things are going to help us here." She pushed herself out of her seat and headed over to one of the stationery tables. Shuffling through their selection of journals, she picked up a soft-cover, navy moleskin notebook, and moved to their pen stand.

"Is a fountain pen getting a bit too carried away?" Jones glanced at Autumn who was still holding the magnifying glass in her hand. She went with the fountain pen.

Back at the table, she opened up the notebook and wrote on the top of the left-hand page 'The Facts' and the top of the opposite page 'Suspects'. She immediately wrote down Candace Chadwick and underlined it heavily.

"The facts." Autumn curled her finger and rested it on her lips. "The fire was started yesterday. What time do you think?"

"Probably around eight or eight-thirty in the morning," said Jones. "The alarm went off just before I opened up for the day."

Autumn nodded. "And do we know how it started?"

Jones shook her head. "Honestly, I know nothing more than, there was a fire, and it was arson."

"So, not a lot to go on."

"Alright how about this," said Jones. She turned the page and titled the next one 'Questions to be answered'.

"We could fill the whole book!" Autumn said.

"Ha ha," said Jones. "How about we just focus on the most

important."

Jones wrote down, 'How was the fire started?' And 'What time did the fire start?'

"Maybe we could check the CFS website?"

Jones quickly brought up her phone. "It says 8:48 am. But that probably means the time they got the call. Not necessarily the time it started."

"Good to note down though." Jones added it to the 'Facts' list. "What I'd like to know is how the police, or the CFS, or whoever it is, knows that it's arson? How do they work that out?"

"Write that down," said Autumn. "Because I have absolutely no idea."

"I feel like I'm writing a feature story on arson," said Jones.

"Maybe you are!"

"You just won't let it go, will you?" said Jones, looking directly at her sister.

"What do you mean?" Autumn furrowed her brow.

"You keep trying to get me to write articles again?"

"Do I?"

"Well, remember you said I should write a review for the Haunted Cellar?"

"And you should!" said Autumn.

"Yes, maybe," said Jones. "But why? Why do you want me to write them?"

"Ah, because you're a journalist!" Autumn wobbled her head before pursing her lips.

Jones sighed. "I know, but it feels like you're trying to push me away. That you want me to go back to Adelaide."

"What!" Autumn rose rapidly, dramatically. "No. No, no, no. I do not want that. Unless that's what you want?"

"That's not the question," said Jones. "The question is, why do you keep wanting me to write the articles? If it isn't to get me to go back to Adelaide?"

"Because you love being a journalist," said Autumn. "That's all! And you can be a journalist in places other than Adelaide. They do have email these days."

Jones rolled her eyes.

"Ok, I'll admit it," said Autumn. "It's all for purely selfish reasons. If you work out a way to do what you love but stay in Lilly Pilly Creek, then I get to keep you!"

Jones laughed. "You get to keep me? Of course, you get to keep me."

"Well, good," said Autumn. "As long as that is clear."

"Crystal."

But what Autumn said did cause her to pause for a moment. It seemed she had gotten it stuck in her head that she had to be in Lilly Pilly Creek running The Memory Bank, or in Adelaide working as a journalist. She hadn't allowed herself to believe that it could be possible to be a journalist *and* run The Memory Bank, all the while staying in Lilly Pilly Creek.

"Someone's at the door," said Autumn. She whizzed away and stuck her head through the wall. "A customer!" she called.

Jones quickly stood, pushing the chair in and taking her notebook and fountain pen over to the counter. She couldn't let that get into the wrong hands.

"Mrs Livingstone! Lovely to see you!" Mrs Livingstone was the very first person Jones ever opened a lockbox for, only a few months ago, days after the grand reopening of The Memory Bank.

"And you Jones," she said. "How are you?"

"Really well," said Jones. "How can I help you?"

"Well, I do have a few things to pop into my lockbox," said Mrs Livingston, holding up a paper bag, before hesitating. "But, well, There was another thing."

"What is it?" asked Jones guiding her into the Bank, and closing the door.

"It's just Sybil said if anyone needed a cool place to stay for a while, well, you were ok with that. Was that right?"

"Of course!" said Jones. "You are very welcome."

"Not today," said Mrs Livingstone. "And not for me. No, it was just, if a fire comes through, well, I'm a bit worried about some of my neighbours. They don't have any family you see."

Jones nodded.

"And of course, they are very welcome at my home," she continued. "But my unit is just too small for everyone."

"I completely understand," said Jones. "Please tell them, they are very welcome to come here. As you can see, we have lots of room. And I have some boxes of water, although I may need to grab some more. Otherwise, there's not much I can offer them."

"That sounds wonderful," said Mrs Livingstone. "I'll let them know and I'm sure they'll pack their own food, and maybe a crossword or a book. I'm just so relieved they will be safe."

"I'm very happy to help," said Jones.

"One word to Sybil and the whole town knows about it!" Autumn called out.

"Well, I'll be off then," said Mrs Livingstone. "I'll go and let the oldies know."

"What about your lockbox?" Jones called after her, but Mrs Livingstone had already closed the door behind her.

Jones shook her head with a smile.

"Sounds like you maybe busy tomorrow," said Autumn. "You might want to get prepared. You could be stuck in here for the day."

"Yes, you might be right," said Jones. "In that case, I think I might join Wren and Mirri for lunch at Hugo's today."

"What, a third wheel?"

"They won't mind!" said Jones. "And if they do, well I'll just hang out with Hugo at the bar."

"Of course you will," said Autumn, smiling.

"Maybe you could do a touch of eavesdropping?" Jones suggested.

"You think the arsonist might be sitting having lunch at Hugo's chatting about it?"

Rolling her eyes, Jones shook her head. "No, I doubt they're that stupid. But you might catch a whiff of the rumour mill."

"And where there's smoke....."

CHAPTER 14

"Jones!" Wren was waving from one of the booths inside Hugo's. "Come and join us!"

"See," Jones said, without glancing at Autumn. "I'm not a third wheel."

"Yet," said Autumn. "Well, you go and have a nice relaxing lunch. I'll be off investigating."

Autumn floated away, gliding towards the bar first, whilst Jones slid in next to Wren, opposite Mirri.

"How was your walking meeting?" Jones asked.

"Solved all the world's problems," said Wren with a wink

"Excellent!" said Jones. "Have you ordered?"

"Not yet, but he's like a bee to honey," said Wren, glancing over Mirri's shoulder.

"Ladies, what can I get you?" smiling at them all, his eyes finally resting on Jones, was Hugo.

After placing their orders, Jones couldn't help but ask him a question. "What are you hearing about the fires?"

"I'm not sure about today's, although I have been keeping an eye on it as it's near my place," he replied.

"But it's going the other way, right?" Jones gulped, realising she had forgotten Hugo's tiny home might be in the path of the fire.

"Yes, for now," said Hugo. "The guys are there at the moment and have told me it's a bit smoky but nothing to worry about."

Jones nodded. "That's good. At least they're keeping an eye on things. And nothing else? No news about what started things."

Hugo caught Jones's eye, and frowned a little, pausing. "Ah, no, nothing has been told directly to me," he shook his head. "You never know with fires. Well, I'd better get these orders in."

Hugo left to grab their sparkling waters, and the three women turned to discuss the fires.

"Is it close to Hugo's?" asked Wren.

"No I don't think so," said Jones. "But Wren, have you ah, have you got any updates on your place?"

"No! I haven't had time. What? Is it close to Lobethal?"

Jones winced, not wanting to be the bearer of any potentially bad news. "Look I don't know, I'm sure it's all ok. But maybe we should check the updates?"

The three of them pulled out their phones and began tapping away, scanning the CFS website before logging into other sites to see what everyone was saying.

"Well, what I'm seeing is that it is more in the vicinity of Kenton Valley, and heading towards Gumeracha," said Mirri.

"That's good, isn't it?" asked Jones. "That's heading away from both you and Hugo."

Wren was nodding. "Yes, it appears so. But still, there are quite a few properties amongst the bushland there. I hope everyone is safe. And here's hoping no one loses their home."

"Actually, I think that's close to Jed's winery, The Haunted Cellar," said Jones. "Gosh, I hope he's ok."

The women frowned but there was nothing to say. Instead, they went back to reading updates on their phones, just to make sure their understanding of the current fire situation was correct. It was hard to sit there knowing another fire was burning, threatening the Hills.

One of the bar staff brought over their drinks which took their attention away from their phones. Jones turned to Mirri. "So, you'll be teaching at the Primary School this year?"

"Yes, I can't wait. I've heard it's a great school," Mirri smiled.

"Where will you live?" asked Jones.

"Oh I rent a place in Balhannah so it's not far. Perfect really."

Balhannah was a small Adelaide Hills town not too far from Lilly Pilly Creek, so her commute to school would be pretty easy.

"Now, Jones," said Wren. "You mentioned something this morning. Or should I say, *didn't* mention something. Can you talk now?"

Jones looked down at her hands and then back to Wren. "Ah, um, well, if you haven't heard anything, then no. No, I can't say anything."

"Gosh, so cryptic!"

Jones knew Wren was teasing, but it was a little frustrating. She was so worried about Atlas and felt powerless. She was also a little angry Christopher seemed to be dragging his feet. Why hadn't someone already phoned Wren? Was he collecting evidence? Hadn't he spoken to Atlas like he said he would? Or maybe he'd found the real culprit and realised that of course Atlas wasn't involved. She could only hope.

"You'll know soon enough," said Jones. Thankfully, she was saved by the arrival of their lunches.

They ate in silence for a while when suddenly it felt as though the whole bar went silent at once. Jones, Wren and Mirri looked at each other and then at everyone in the room. They were all on their phones.

"What's going on?" hissed Mirri.

"It's the fire," Jones heard Autumn say. "It's headed this way!"

Jones hurriedly dropped her knife and fork on her plate, clattering loudly, and grabbed her phone.

"Oh, no," she said.

"What!" Wren grabbed Jones's phone out of her hand.

"The fire," said Jones. "It's heading towards Lilly Pilly Creek."

"Surely not!" said Mirri. "It's too far away for that, right?"

Wren was reading as quickly as she could. "It's not close yet," she explained. "But the wind has changed. It appears it's going to miss Lobethal but Jones is right. The wind is pushing the fire this way."

"What should we do?" asked Mirri, her eyes wide.

"Well, if I were you two, I'd be heading directly to Balhannah," said Jones. "You'll be well out of the way."

"Yes," said Mirri, quickly turning to Wren. "You should come to my place. It won't be safe to go home."

"But Jones said it was going to miss Lobethal," said Wren, pursing her lips.

Jones shook her head. "You shouldn't risk it, Wren. And you don't want to get in the way of all the fire trucks."

"Jones is right," said Mirri. "Come on Wren, come back to my place, and you can go home as soon as we are sure it is safe."

Wren sighed, resigned. "Can I at least finish my lunch?"

Mirri smiled at her girlfriend. "Of course," she said.

Jones couldn't help but smile at the two of them. They were very comfortable with each other and quite protective.

"What will you do, Jones?" Wren asked.

"I'll go back to The Memory Bank," she said.

"You can't do that!" Fury flashed across Wren's face. "The fire is literally headed this way!"

Jones shook her head. "I can't leave," she tried to explain. "The Memory Bank will be one of the safest places if the fire does come this far. I have to stay. People are counting on me."

"Who?" asked Wren, frowning. "Who is counting you?"

"The town," said Jones. "I told Sybil that anyone who had nowhere else to go could come to The Memory Bank."

"What did you do that for?" Wren scoffed at Jones. Wren couldn't possibly understand. She had no idea that no matter what, she would never leave Autumn.

Yet, it appeared her sister was on Wren's side. "I know you're only staying because of me," said Autumn, who appeared behind Mirri. "But you really should go with Wren."

"Look, I'm staying, and there is nothing you can say," said Jones, to both Wren and Autumn. "I'll be safe. I'll look after myself."

Jones saw Wren go to open her mouth, but Mirri shook her head. Somehow Mirri sensed there was nothing more Wren could say.

Wren shoved the last mouthful in her mouth and finished her drink. "Well, you know you can always come to Mirri's. Right?"

"Absolutely," said Mirri. "Please Jones, you are welcome any time."

"Thank you Mirri," Jones said. "If it gets dangerous, I promise I'll leave." She glanced up at Autumn, and then across to Hugo who was wiping glasses behind the bar. Most people appeared to be leaving, realising they needed to get to safety.

Jones hugged Wren and the Mirri quickly followed, pulling Jones in for a hug. They said their goodbyes, Wren again insisting Jones come with them before Mirri pulled her out the door.

"What are you going to do?" Jones asked Hugo, taking a seat at the bar in front of him.

Hugo shook his head. "I'm not sure. I've just had Chappy on the phone and they can see smoke from my place. I told them to leave."

"Where will they go?"

"I told them to go home," Hugo said. "But of course they're insisting on coming here, to make sure everything is ok."

"What do they think they can do?"

"Help me, help the bar, help Lilly Pilly Creek," he said. "These guys might not look it, but they are all very good in an emergency."

Jones nodded, sipping her drink. Chappy and Rusty she could see might be capable of pulling together in a crisis. But Phoneix? He didn't strike her as the type to rally and pitch in.

"You know you are all welcome at The Memory Bank," said Jones.

"So you're going to stay?" Hugo asked. He glanced at her and then back down at the glass he was drying, not giving away his opinion.

Jones nodded. "I'll be safe at The Memory Bank," she said. "I have a feeling a few people are going to come and take refuge there. I've offered it to them."

Hugo smiled at her. "Well, I'll stay at the bar as long as I can and I'll come to the Bank if I need to. Or if you need me. You know you just have to ask."

Jones nodded and smiled. "I know," she said, reaching out and squeezing his hand. "Thank you. I'd better get back and open up again. People might be waiting."

Before she left, Hugo stepped out from behind the bar and gave her a long hug. Although they weren't panicking, the two of them realised this felt different. The fire was moving in their direction and they had to be prepared.

CHAPTER 15

Stepping outside, Jones was surprised how strong the smell of smoke was.

"Can you see anything?" Jones asked Autumn who was currently flying towards her from above Hugo's.

"Just a lot of smoke," said Autumn. "But it looks a long way away."

"It smells a lot closer," said Jones, walking towards The Memory Bank. Standing there was Mr Manowski, Mrs Livingstone, and a small group of elderly men and women.

"Jones!" said Mrs Livingstone. "Thanks goodness. I thought maybe you had changed your mind."

Jones shook her head and smiled. "No, of course not. I was just having lunch at Hugo's when the news came through." She pulled out her key and unlocked the front door. "Come in, come in." She keyed in the alarm code and flicked the light switch, before turning to help the party of guests. There were a couple of eskys on wheels, some deck chairs, and even a card table.

"You've all come prepared!" Jones said.

"Oh, we're just so thankful you'll have us," said a woman carrying the card table. "I couldn't bear sitting at home by myself wondering what was going to happen."

"But, remember the plan!" said Mrs Livingstone sounding like a school teacher.

"The plan?" said Jones.

"This is just a safer place than home," she explained. "If the fire does threaten Lilly Pilly Creek we'll all be jumping in my car and Mr Manowski's and heading to the Bushfire Refuge in Mylor."

"Yes, that is a very smart idea," said Jones. "But for now, at least everyone is together, in a cool place, and we can all look after each other."

"Where would you like us to set up," asked a tall, thin man, pulling a large orange esky on wheels.

Jones opened her arms wide. "Wherever you like! I doubt any customers will come in, and if they do, well they can just move around you."

"We'll keep out of the way," said the man, before turning to his friends. "Come on, let's head over here." He led them towards the garden glass doors where there was an area free of display tables and bookshelves. Jones suspected he wanted a good vantage point to view the outside. The woman flipped open her card table, and others fiddled with their deck chairs, managing to get them up with some difficulty. It appeared they had everything they needed and were very self-sufficient. Jones almost laughed when one woman pulled out some martini glasses and asked if anyone wanted a gin and tonic. She even had olives!

Jones left them to it. With Autumn by her side, Jones made her way around The Memory Bank, ensuring all the windows were closed, in an attempt to keep the smoke from seeping in. The garden doors were closed but not locked, just in case anyone needed to make an emergency entry or exit.

"I think the next thing we need to do is to research arson," said Autumn.

"Really?" said Jones. "Don't you think that might look a bit suspicious? What if the police decide to search my computer?"

"First of all, why would they?" asked Autumn. "And secondly, did you do any arson research before the first fire? Or the second for that matter?"

Jones scoffed. "Of course not!"

"Well, then you have nothing to worry about."

Jones walked into one of the rear meeting rooms and shut the door. "So what exactly do you want me to search for?

"I'd personally like to understand what type of people commit arson," said Autumn. "I bet there's lots of research done on that. It might help us narrow down the suspects."

"But don't you think the police will be doing this? I'm sure they have expert arson investigators."

"Of course!" said Autumn, seating herself opposite Jones. "All the more reason for us to investigate."

Jones raised her eyebrows. "Are you worried they might find a way to pin it on Atlas?" she asked.

Autumn shrugged. "Aren't you?"

Jones put her head in her hands before looking back up. "I'm really worried. But I also feel ridiculous, because how could they possibly think it was Atlas?"

"It's like Christopher said," said Autumn. "It's often someone involved with actually fighting the fires, isn't it? So of course Atlas would be on a suspect list."

"That's what they say," said Jones. "But just because Atlas is the newest on the crew, doesn't mean they have to automatically point the finger at him. They seem to have lasered in on him. We need to find out more about this Candace woman. I mean how dare she suggest Atlas as the culprit!"

Autumn was nodding her head furiously. "I agree! Who is she to name Atlas? She doesn't even know him! Anyone who knew Atlas would never in a million years suggest he could deliberately start a fire."

"It's just as likely to be her," said Jones. "And she's setting him up."

Autumn moaned. "But who's going to believe Atlas over the Crew Captain?"

The sisters fell silent. Jones had her eyes closed and was rubbing her eyebrows. Autumn began to slowly float upwards, as though her deep contemplation meant her body had forgotten about gravity.

What if Autumn was right? If the only real suspect the police had was Atlas, then it was going to be very hard for him. They would have no evidence, of course. But if the whole of Lilly Pilly Creek was led to believe he was responsible, Atlas would be sentenced by the community anyway. Poor Atlas. They would not leave him to fight this alone.

"We *are* going to have to investigate," sighed Jones. "Aren't we? I mean unless Christopher has discovered who the real arsonist is, we're going to have to find some sort of evidence that exonerates Atlas."

Autumn floated back down and locked eyes with her sister. "Until Atlas is proven innocent, we need to do anything we can to help him."

At that moment, Jones's phone beeped indicating a message had come through. It was from Wren.

I've just had the phone call you were expecting. Meeting A at the station now.

"Oh no," said Jones, shaking her head.

"What?" asked Autumn.

Jones pushed the phone over so her sister could read it.

"For goodness sake!" exclaimed Autumn. "Christopher better watch his step."

"I'm sure Christopher will do everything by the book," said Jones. "It's not him I'm worried about."

"Who are you worried about?"

"I have a feeling Atlas will be interviewed by someone outside of Lilly Pilly Creek. Someone who specialises in arson," said Jones.

"Someone who doesn't know Atlas from a bar of soap," said Autumn.

"Exactly."

"I'm going over there!" cried out Autumn.

"No, you're not!"

"Why not? I should get ahead of the investigation. Get all the information I can."

Jones shook her head. "No, you can't. I'm sorry, but I feel that is taking things a step too far."

Autumn stared at her sister for a moment before dropping her shoulders. "You're right," she said. "We can't eavesdrop on a friend like this. But are you sure? Don't you think we're doing it for the right reasons?"

The pair were silent for a moment before they both frowned and shook their heads. They understood they couldn't cross a line like this. However, that didn't mean they wouldn't do everything else they could for Atlas. It was up to them.

CHAPTER 16

The Memory Bank was quiet that afternoon. At least in terms of customers. The guests taking refuge were getting rowdier as the afternoon wore on. It appeared the gin and tonic was well and truly flowing.

Amidst the storytelling and cackling, there was the constant melody of sirens in the distance. It was unlike anything Jones had heard before.

Hugo popped in a few times during the afternoon, sharing updates and checking on Jones.

"We're all fine in here," Jones laughed, looking pointedly at the group who currently had all eyes on a man who was dramatically acting out a story. "No customers of course. How about you?"

Hugo grinned and shook his head. "Nope. A couple popped in to grab some wine to tide them over, but until this fire is under control, I think we're going to be pretty quiet. I do have the boys keeping me company though."

"So they've left your place? That's good."

"I told them to get out of there," he explained. "No point risking their lives for my little house."

"You're right," said Jones, wrapping her arm around his waist. "But it is a gorgeous little house. I hope nothing happens to it."

Hugo bent down and pecked Jones on the lips. "Well, I'd better get back in there. I have a feeling my guests are getting nearly as raucous as yours."

Jones hugged him before watching him leave.

"Oh, he's worried about you," said Autumn, playfully fluttering her eyelashes as she floated back to her sister.

"I'm sure he'd be worried about you too *if* he knew you existed," said Jones, who perched herself up at the counter to continue googling arsonists. It seemed the rabble to the left was so engrossed in the stories they were telling each other they didn't notice Jones talking to her invisible sister.

"Of course, I'm sure he would be. So, have you found out anything?" asked Autumn, pointing at the computer.

"Well, psychologists say that arsonists are more likely to have some sort of mental health issue," responded Jones, reading from the screen. "They're most likely to be male, socially isolated, and lack coping skills."

"Well, Atlas only meets one of those criteria, wouldn't you say?"

"What, being male?" asked Jones. "I don't know anything about his mental health, but I wouldn't say he was socially isolated or lacking coping skills. Would you?"

"Not at all," said Autumn. "But does that mean it's unlikely to be a woman who sets fires? Unlikely to be someone like Candace?"

Jones scrolled down the page she was reading and then shook her head. "No, not at all. Up to one-third of firesetters, as they call them, can be female. I'd say that's a rather high percentage, so I don't think this rules out either gender."

Autumn nodded, staring off into the distance.

"Here's where we might run into problems," said Jones. "I've just found another article which says an arsonist is most likely to be less than twenty-five years old, unmarried, and living with their parents."

"Atlas meets all of those!" said Autumn.

"I know," sighed Jones. "But wait a moment. It also says that the father is likely not living in the home, that they have a domineering mother, that they are disabled in some way and have a feeling of inadequacy or insecurity. That doesn't sound like Atlas, does it?"

"Absolutely not!"

"But who does it sound like?" asked Jones.

Autumn raised her eyebrows. "Well, I know nothing about this Phoenix guy, but I bet we'd find out he met many of those characteristics."

"Just not twenty-five years old," said Jones. "I think he's in his late thirties. He was named after River Phoenix from Stand By Me."

"Yes," said Autumn. "Late thirties sounds right. But if that's the only thing he doesn't tick on that list, then he should be looked at closely. Do you think you should say something to Christopher?"

Jones took a deep breath. "Not until I speak to Hugo first. And the thought of doing that makes me feel sick."

"It'll be alright," said Autumn. "Hugo's a sensible guy. Surely he would understand what you were saying."

"Perhaps," said Jones. "But in the meantime, do we have any other suspects? Because I don't think Candace Chadwick meets many of those possible personality traits."

"But we don't know anything about her," said Autumn. "Perhaps we need to suss her out a bit more?"

"So currently our suspects are Phoenix and Candace. Is there anyone else?"

The two sisters were silent for a few minutes, thinking. But they were soon interrupted.

"Jones!" Hugo was calling across the room. "Jones, I think you need to tell your guests to make a move."

Jones's eyes widened. "What's going on?"

"The fire," said Hugo. "It's getting closer. It's headed straight for us."

"Oh no!" cried out Autumn.

Jones ran directly over to the group and told them what Hugo had said. "Shall I ring Mrs Livingstone and Mr Manowski?"

"It's ok Jones dear," said one of the ladies. "We have a signal. I'll just text them both and they'll be on their way." The elderly woman pulled out her phone and deftly typed in her message. "Right everyone, let's pack up so we're ready to go!"

The group stood, finishing any last drops in their drinks, before folding, stacking and packing.

Watching the group transform from a rabble to a high-functioning team left Jones speechless. Maybe they hadn't consumed as many gins as she'd thought.

"What are you going to do, Jones?" Hugo asked.

"Oh, I'm staying here," she replied.

"You must go to Mirri's!" cried Autumn.

"Well, if you're sure," said Hugo. "Then I'll stay here with you."

"Don't listen to her Hugo!" Autumn yelled. "Tell her to go to

Mirri's house!"

"Yes, that would be nice," said Jones, ignoring her sister.

"But I will need to invite the fellas. Is that ok?"

"Of course, of course," said Jones. "Although won't they just ride home? It might be safer?"

"Those blokes couldn't care less about being safe. They want to be in the centre of the action. They'll be useful if we need help."

Jones smiled and nodded at Hugo, although it did cross her mind that of course, Phoenix wanted to stay in town, to witness the results of his handiwork.

"That sounds great," said Jones. "Bring them over whenever you like. I'll be fine here. I'm going to go and turn the sprinklers on in the garden, and start putting wet towels around the place."

"Well, leave something for me to do," said Hugo. "I'll go and check on the bar and send all the staff home. Then I'll be back. I suppose you won't say no to me bringing over some wine too?"

"Absolutely not!' Jones grinned.

Hugo walked out the door just as Mrs Livingstone and Mr Manowski walked in.

"The cavalry is here!" called Mrs Livingstone grandly. Mr Manowski smiled, walking over to pick up an esky and the card table.

"I'm not quite sure how much gin they've all had," Jones confided in Mrs Livingstone.

"Got a bit raucous, did they?"

Jones grinned. "Nothing we couldn't handle. They've certainly made the most of their predicament!"

Mrs Livingstone patted Jones on the arm. "Thank you so much," she said. "It was certainly a weight off my mind, knowing they were here. I just hope this fire doesn't get as close as they're saying. The wind has really picked up out there."

Jones glanced out the window and saw gum trees twisting and bending in the distance. It was the first time she had paused and thought about how serious things were getting.

"You know you should be leaving," called out Autumn. "You should go with them!"

Jones gave Autumn a side eye but ignored her. "Here's hoping the CFS can handle it. There sure are a lot of sirens."

Mr Manowski came over and held out his hand to Jones. "Thank you for looking after them," he said, shaking her hand.

"I didn't really do much, but at least they were all together," she replied. "Hopefully they'll all be back in their own beds tonight."

Mr Manowski nodded a frown on his face. Jones realised he didn't believe that would be the case.

"Good luck Jones," Mr Manowski said.

"Don't wait until it's too late," Mrs Livingstone called, leading the group to the front door.

There was a chorus of thank you as the group stepped into the furnace outside.

"You really should leave," said Autumn, gliding up next to her. "I'd die if anything happened to you."

Both of them ignored the play on words.

"Not a chance," said Jones shaking her head.

There was no way she was leaving her sister again.

CHAPTER 17

"Oh no," said Jones. "We never checked the generator!"

Jones had pulled out her bushfire plan and was working her way through the list. She had towels soaking in the bathroom sinks, wetting them again as an extra precaution. She took the dripping piles through The Memory Bank, rolling them and pressing them up against the bottom of external doors, and on top of window sills.

"I think you're just going to have to hope for the best," said Autumn.

'What, that the power doesn't go off?"

Autumn nodded. "You may just have to manage."

Jones sighed, annoyed at herself. She realised she had gotten too caught up in the mystery of the arsonist, instead of concentrating on what was important. Helping the town and saving The Memory Bank.

"Perhaps I should call Rex?"

"I guess you could try," said Autumn. "He may have evacuated though."

A ping noise came from her phone. Jones read aloud.

Watch and Act. Leave Now. Issued for Lilly Pilly Creek. Take action now as this bushfire may threaten your safety. If you are not prepared, leave now and if the path is clear, go to a safer place. Do not enter this area as conditions are dangerous.

"This is your last chance," said Autumn. "Don't you think you should leave? Go and take Hugo and his mates, and go to Mirri's. I'll be fine."

Jones just shook her head, returning to the bathroom for another armful of wet towels. She didn't say a word to her sister.

"Ugh! You're so stubborn!" moaned Autumn. "This is what you've always been like. Stubborn. Always your way or the highway. We're so different!" She flew to the ceiling and then whipped around in a series of figure eights.

Jones stopped and turned to watch her sister, surprised at this outburst.

"Where is this coming from?" asked Jones.

"It's just so frustrating! You won't listen to anything I say. You never do!" She was now holding onto an arm of the chandelier.

"I'm here aren't I!" cried Jones. "I'm running the Bank when I should be the one out there, reporting on the fires! I wouldn't call that stubborn."

"If that's what you want to do then go!" Autumn returned fire. "I know you'd rather be out there chasing the story. Instead of stuck here with me. And still, you're willing to put yourself at risk just to get your own way."

"Get my own way! You know that's not why I'm staying. Don't you dare say that," Jones went so far as to stomp her foot and put her hands on her hips. How could Autumn not understand?

"Well, then why? Why on earth are you still here?"

"For you!" said Jones, groaning. "Everything is for you! I couldn't bear it if I left and when I got back you were gone again."

"What makes you think I'll be gone? How is a fire going to affect me? It just goes straight through me!"

"How do you know? You don't know that? You haven't walked through flames. What if the fire does something to your energy? Sucks it away?"

"Is that what you think?" Autumn's voice was much quieter now. "You truly think that if Lilly Pilly Creek is engulfed in fire it could take me away?"

"Of course I do," said Jones. "Of course, I'm worried about you. How could I live if you weren't here anymore?"

Autumn slowly floated down from the ceiling and hovered in front of Jones. "But you know it's going to happen eventually. Right? You know I'm not going to be here forever?"

"How do I know that? You don't know that? Neither of us knows what's going to happen to you."

"But Jones, it doesn't mean you should stop living your life. I'm the one that's dead. Not you. You can't keep placing yourself in danger for me. You can't keep holding onto The Memory Bank for me if it's not what you truly want to do." Autumn's face was sad and desperate.

"I'm exactly where I want to be. I am doing what I want to do. I'm fine Autumn," Jones explained.

"But what if I'm not?"

"What on earth are you talking about?" Now Jones was very confused.

"What if I'm not happy with you here?"

"You don't want me to run The Memory Bank?" Jones asked, eyes bulging, surprised by what Autumn was saying. "I know I'm not doing it like you would have if you were alive. But I thought things were going well. I thought you were happy?"

"Of course I'm happy," said Autumn. "I'm thrilled with everything you've done. The Memory Bank is much better because of you. That's not what I meant. I meant that I'm not happy that I'm the one holding you back. For some unknown reason, I'm stuck here, a ghost, and you've turned your life upside down because of it."

"Because I wanted to," said Jones. "I want to be here. I want to be here with you. I want to run The Memory Bank. No, I didn't expect it to happen this way, for my life to take this direction. But this is where I'm meant to be right now."

"But don't you think you should be out there with Quinn? Instead of Quinn? Shouldn't you be writing these stories?"

"Perhaps," shrugged Jones. "But in the last few years, I rarely covered stories like this. Quinn is the right person to be doing it. I will admit it is nice to have her here, so I can experience that rush again through her. But it's not like I'd be in her place if I wasn't living in Lilly Pilly Creek. I'd probably be sitting in the newsroom, working on something much less exciting."

"But you could go out and join Quinn? If you wanted to. I'm sure she'd appreciate your help."

Jones laughed. "I'm not so sure about that. I think Quinn is very much a solo operator."

Autumn had to nod in agreement. "I think you're right." Then, more quietly. "So there's nothing I can say? Nothing to convince you to put your safety above mine?"

Jones shook her head. "Not at all. The two of us, together, will face this fire. I think there's one thing above all that we can agree on. We are so much better together."

Autumn smiled, nodding, tears glistening on her eyelashes. "Yes. Why did it take us so long to realise it?"

"Why did it take your death to bring us back together?"

The sisters smiled at each other, tears rolling down their cheeks.

Then the doors to The Memory Bank were pushed open.

CHAPTER 18

Hugo had arrived with Chappy, Rusty and Phoenix. They were carrying boxes and bags, and one towed an esky in. Jones hurriedly turned her face, wiping away the tears before walking over to the group.

"What's all of this?" asked Jones, trying to subtly ensure no tears remained, as Hugo led the boys to one of the tables where customers usually sat.

"All the sustenance we should require," Hugo said, smiling. "If you're hungry or thirsty, just grab whatever you need." He waved his hand with a flourish in the direction of the supplies they had brought.

"He is a knight in shining armour," said Autumn, who had somehow fashioned a ghostly swing that was hanging by a long rope from the ceiling. She glided back and forth, watching the preparations going on below.

Jones had to agree. She certainly didn't mind having a boyfriend who swept in delivering food and drinks, and everything they might need to hunker down whilst they awaited the fire front. After the tears she had shed with Autumn only a few moments ago, she was on the brink of bursting into full-scale sobbing. Instead, she took a deep breath, rolled her shoulders back, and returned to grab the last armful of damp towels.

At that moment, there was a loud banging on the doors, before it was hurriedly opened. Almost tumbling in were Colin Fletcher, Rex Keenan and Mr Kwok, all with their t-shirts pulled over their nose and mouths.

"Oh good, you're here!" cried Rex. "We're too late to leave. You don't mind if we stay here until everything calms down?"

Jones nodded and smiled. "Not at all. The more the merrier. Come in, come in."

"We've brought plenty of food and grog!" called out Rusty "Get over here and help us out!" Jones appreciated that Rusty felt comfortable with these strangers.

Colin and Mr Kwok dutifully joined the blokes in getting drinks on ice, opening packets of chips, and pouring peanuts into bowls. Chappy was even rather deftly laying out a cheese platter.

Jones managed to grab Rex. "Rex, I've been a bit stupid."

"Oh?" he cocked his head to one side.

"The thing is, I believe The Memory Bank has a generator, but I've completely forgotten to check it. I have no idea if it works, and now I'm worried we're going to lose power."

Rex smiled. "It's ok Jones," he said. "To be honest I hope it's not working. If it's filled with petrol it would be quite the fire hazard if you haven't prepped the area properly."

"Oh no! I didn't even think of that," said Jones, her chest filling with panic.

"Don't worry, Jones," said Rex. "I'll run out and take a look."

Jones was relieved Rex had arrived. She was sure he would put her mind at ease. She went to grab a mop and fixed up the drips she had left all over the Bank's timber floors. As she was finishing up, the front door was flung open again.

103

"Oh, everyone's here!" cried Prue who burst in along with, to Jone's surprise, Wren.

"Wren! What are you doing here?"

"I had to drop my *client* home, and by the time I got back to Lilly Pilly Creek on my way to Balhannah, they told us it was too late to leave. I spotted Prue on the street, and I told her you wouldn't mind if we came here."

"Of course, of course," Jones scooped them both into the Bank and then shut the door, leaving the heat and smoke on the other side.

"You have quite the crowd!" said Prue. "I've brought wine. That's all I had in the office sorry." Jones laughed, knowing how much wine they already had.

"Why didn't you get out earlier, Prue?" asked Jones.

"You know me," said Prue. "I just kept working, thinking I had plenty of time. I'd sent everyone else home hours ago. Stupid I guess. I was heading back to my house when Wren waved me down."

"I knew they wouldn't let her through," said Wren. "I'd already been turned around, so thought I'd save her the hassle."

Knowing Prue, Jones thought that was particularly gracious of Wren. Jones wondered if she might have let Prue find out for herself.

"Well come in," said Jones. "Add the wine to the selection. Hugo has the food sorted."

The three women walked to the table where Hugo was adding quince paste and olives to the already delectable platter. It was laid with blue cheese, dried pear, triple cream brie, olives and prosciutto as well as cheddar curd.

"This looks amazing!" said Jones.

"Oh you have to try the cheese," said Hugo. "It's from the new cheesery that's opening soon. Butternut. I've been trialling these in the bar."

Hugo handed her a seed cracker topped with the triple cream brie and quince paste. It was oozing slightly and as she placed it in her mouth, the creamy tang was delicious.

"This is amazing," said Jones.

"All made from Adelaide Hills milk," explained Hugo.

Wren and Prue helped themselves whilst Hugo's friends handed out drinks to everyone.

"Well, if we have to ride out a bush fire, I suppose this is the way to do it," said Wren.

Jones laughed, but couldn't help glancing out the windows. The light was starting to turn an eerie orange. The air was hazy which distorted the branches of the gum trees that were bending chaotically in the wind.

Jones quickly pulled Wren aside and asked her about Atlas.

"He's fine," said Wren. "Christopher said it all looked good. He didn't have a clear alibi, but that's because he was the only one home the morning of the fire. But I'm sure Christopher knows it wasn't him. He said he may need to talk to him again, but they had no concrete evidence, and if the CFS needed him, he was allowed back at the firefront."

"Oh no," said Jones.

"I thought that would be good news?" said Wren.

"It is, it is," said Jones. "I just worry about Atlas being so close to the fires. The only good thing to come of him being accused of arson was that he was away from the danger."

"That's true," said Wren, putting her arm around her friend. "I also want you to know that he wasn't *really* accused of arson. It's just that Candace had to share with the police who the newest recruits were. It's part of the process that anyone new is looked at closely. Unfortunately, this time it just happens to be Atlas."

"Poor Atlas," said Jones before walking over to stand next to Hugo. As she brought her attention back to the group she saw Autumn waving at her from the bottom of the spiral staircase. It was clear she wanted Jones to follow her up the stairs.

"I'm just going to head up to the tower and see if I can spot anything," said Jones to Hugo.

"Do you want me to come?" asked Hugo. He looked at her, concerned, which was understandable. The last time Hugo had been up those stairs, he was rescuing Jones from Autumn's crazed ex-boyfriend as he was about to push Jones down the staircase, just as he had done to her sister.

Jones smiled and nodded. "I'll be fine, thanks."

As Jones reached the bottom of the stairs, Autumn turned and floated ahead. Jones made her way up, slowly, watching every step as she always did.

As she reached the top she could smell smoke. There were gaps in the tower she hadn't thought to block with towels.

"You get the best view from this window over here." Autumn was indicating the window directly opposite the clock face. Peering out Jones could see was a wall of billowing dark grey smoke in the distance. When she looked lower she spotted red flames shooting up into the air. It was still a way from Lilly Pilly Creek, but with the high temperatures and strong winds, she knew it would be moving quickly.

"What are we going to do?" Jones turned to Autumn.

"Nothing," said Autumn. "There's nothing more we can do except hope the CFS can save the town."

They both went quiet and could hear the sirens of fire trucks in the distance. She could only imagine how many crews, from all around the state, were being called in to help them.

"I'm honestly starting to get scared now," Jones said.

"Of course you are," said Autumn. "But Hugo and your friends are here. And I'm here. It will be ok."

Autumn's manner had turned from angry and frantic to mothering and calm. They both knew, as Wren had told them, that there was nowhere Jones could go. It was up to The Memory Bank to protect her and her friends now.

"I'll keep watch," said Autumn. "You go back downstairs. If there's anything you should know, I'll call out."

"Why don't you come down too?" asked Jones.

"I'd rather be up here keeping lookout than watching you all enjoy the wine and cheese."

Jones looked up at her sister, startled, but then found her sister grinning at her. Autumn winked.

Jones smiled. "Alright, well let me know if anything changes.

Anything at all."

"Of course," said Autumn. "Go down, be with Hugo. Look after each other."

Jones made her way slowly down the stairs. She smiled as she turned the final bend and saw Hugo watching her. He grinned, stood, and brought over a glass of wine.

"Spot anything out there?" he asked.

"A heck of a lot of smoke," said Jones. "And I could see some flames in the distance."

"Really?" Hugo appeared genuinely surprised.

"Yes, although they seemed a long way away."

"It's pretty windy out there though," said Hugo. "Let's hope the CFS have it under control before it gets to the town."

Hugo took her hand and led her over to the group.

Despite the danger they were all in, it was quite fun to spend time with some of her closest friends. Not to mention a past nemesis in Prue, and Hugo's own friends, chatting, drinking and eating. As everyone was doing their best to distract each other, the storytelling was reaching great heights. It seemed, to Jones's surprise, more than one person had a fire-related story to share. As Jones watched Hugo and his mates share some of their escapades, riding motorbikes through a desert in the current retelling, she remembered she had been interrupted the last time she went to ask them how they all met. She wanted to know the answer to that question but decided now was probably not the time. For some reason, she was apprehensive about finding out. Maybe that discussion was best had in private with Hugo.

After a few more glasses of wine and beer and a lot more cheese, everyone's eyes turned to Phoenix, who had decided it was finally his turn to speak.

CHAPTER 19

Phoenix didn't make eye contact with anyone. He looked at his hands, the lighter he always seemed to hold, cupped in his palm. He wasn't flicking the wheel this time. But he did stare at the silver item.

It didn't take long for Jones to realise Phoenix was telling a ghost story. Autumn must have worked this out too, because, unbeknownst to everyone else, she slowly slid down behind Phoenix, before floating around and taking a seat on The Memory Bank's counter directly opposite him.

Jones wondered if ghost stories were always this common, or did she start to attract them to her, now that she had a ghost by her side?

"I worked on a shearing crew," he explained. "For a time I travelled from station to station, shearing thousands of sheep. It was hard work. You were always dirty and tired, and your muscles and back never stopped aching. But I always knew exactly what was expected of me every day. I knew I'd get decent food, and the morning teas were usually exceptional. They know how to cook real food out bush."

Jones and Hugo smiled, raising their eyebrows. Clearly, a fancy cheese platter wasn't to Phoenix's taste.

"Well, the thing with stations is there's always shearer's quarters. Some are better than others. Some are newer than others. But on a couple of the stations you're staying in the same shearer's quarters that were built in the 1800's. So we're talking old. And to be honest, I reckon some of the beds they made us sleep on were that old too."

The group laughed at this, and Phoneix even dared to glance up at his audience, very briefly, appreciating their involvement.

"Well, this one station, it was called Wirri Nirri Downs, and I only ever went there once. It was a place everyone knew, and now, if I mention to shearers, especially the old-timers, with the right tone of voice, they'll mumble under their breath, and nod their head, and I know I don't need to say any more. I know they've seen exactly what I'm about to tell you."

The group all seemed to inhale at the same time. Jones had to give it to Phoenix, he was good at creating tension. Even if it turned out this whole story was a fairytale, he was delivering it like a pro.

"The set up of these shearer's quarters was different to most others. Usually, you had two or more fellas in a room. But this one, there were two huge dorms, and then there were five rooms down one end that only had one bed each. I was told these used to be where they sent anyone who was sick, to keep away from the rest of the team. Maybe they still did that. But this time round, no one was sick, and it was just luck of the draw that I got a single room. The one right at the far end. I was pretty happy with myself. A room all to myself for a week or more. Luck was on my side." Phoenix paused. "Or so I thought."

The crowd all started glancing at each other, not able to guess what he was about to say.

"The first few nights were fine," said Phoenix. "Had the best sleep I'd had in months. And that meant I was shearing personal best numbers each day. It seemed like Wirrie Nirri Downs was my lucky place. Then on the fourth night, everything changed."

Phoenix paused, and now he took to snapping his lighter, letting the flint spark, the fire glow for a moment, before letting it go out. He repeated this over and over before resuming his story.

"There was no moon on the fourth night. I remember trying to find the dunny, and cursing that I'd forgotten my torch."

Everyone laughed at this, and even Phoenix managed a bit of a grin as he remembered it, still looking at his hands. Then his face returned to serious. He frowned, silent for what felt like minutes.

"I was back in bed for only a few minutes when I heard the handle of my door turn."

The crowd was silent, listening to every word.

"'Wrong room!' I called out, without looking up. I was waiting for someone to apologise and the door to close, but it never did. 'What's up?' I asked, leaning up on my side and looking towards the door. It was wide open, and standing in the doorway was a dark shadow. 'Oi, whaddaya doing?' No one answered. But the dark shape moved. Towards me, towards the bed. I was blinking furiously, trying to see who it was. I quickly sat up, leaning up against the end of the bed. The air had turned cold, and suddenly I knew this wasn't a human."

Jones gasped before glancing at Hugo who had a slight grin on his face.

"Bloody hell," Jones heard Autumn say. "I *am not* living my potential as a ghost."

Jones desperately wanted to laugh but knew realised it would be utterly out of place given the mood of the room. Everyone else was glancing around and murmuring under their breath.

"I could barely take a breath," said Phoenix. "The being, whatever it was, sat down on the end of the bed. I could feel the weight of them. I couldn't move. I daren't move. Whenever I've thought about it since I honestly don't think I could if I tried. It was like it had some sort of power over me. It was controlling me."

Jones looked at the people around her. Wren's eyes were wide, her hand clamped over her mouth as though to muffle a scream. Prue had her hands clenched in front of her, her knuckles white. Rex and Colin were expressionless, but taking numerous swigs of their beer. Hugo and his mates were listening but weren't as frightened. They must have heard this story before. However, Jones noted they were taking things seriously. It seemed at least from their point of view, Phoenix was telling the truth.

"It was at the moment that I was sure I saw yellow eyes. Human shaped, but yellow."

Phoenix waited to let everyone take in this information.

"This is my room." Phoenix's voice was deep, playing the part of the ghost. "Leave."

"I'm not going to lie," said Phoenix in his own voice. "I squealed like a little girl."

The whole group bust out laughing. Phoenix was grinning as he continued.

"I grabbed everything of mine, threw it out the door, and got as far away from that room as possible. I ended up sleeping on the floor of a dorm. Worst sleep of my life, but it was better than coming face-to-face with that thing again."

"Far out," said Prue. "Did you tell anyone about it?"

Phoenix shook his head. "Not for months and months. But then one day I met an old shearer at a pub in Broken Hill, and I just mentioned Wirri Nirri in passing. He looked me in the eyes, and I knew he knew."

Phoenix flicked his eyes up to the group before looking back at his hands.

"I asked him questions. The story goes that years ago there'd been a bushfire out there on that station. Instead of shearing, the fellas had been fighting off the fire all day. They didn't have much water to hand so they were using grain sacks to whack it down. At one point the wind changed and a few fellas almost got caught. They all raced to the trucks and headed back to the homestead. There was nothing more they could do. It wasn't until dinner time that they realised one of them was missing."

Colin grunted, and others groaned.

"And the ghost was him?" Wren asked.

Phoenix nodded. "They searched for hours but it was impossible in the dark to find him. The biggest surprise was to come. They found him dead in his bed, my bed, the next day. He'd crawled on his hands and knees all the way back, but he was too exhausted and had suffered too many burns, that he couldn't alert anyone. He died in the very room I had slept in."

Phoenix lifted his head and stared directly into Jones's eyes. "It seems he has never left."

Jones felt her body erupt in goosebumps. Why had he locked eyes with her? Did he know? Jones kept her eyes on his. Was it that he could see ghosts, all ghosts? Could he see Autumn? Jones gripped her right thumb with her left hand, willing herself not to glance in Autumn's direction.

"Wow, that's an amazing story," Jones forced herself to say something. "You said you still had a few days to go at that Station. Did you stay?"

"Not a chance," Phoenix shook his head and looked back down at his hands. "I stayed one more night in my swag and then when the mail plane flew in I jumped on that and got the hell out of there. Usually, this would have caused a big hoo-ha, but when I mentioned where I'd been sleeping, the station manager just nodded his head and slapped my shoulder goodbye."

CHAPTER 20

The storytelling moved on and Jones sat back, listening, but not as intently as before. Instead, she closely watched the group of people in front of her, including Phoenix. She especially watched his gaze, to see if she spotted him tracking Autumn at any point. However, aside from glancing occasionally at a fellow storyteller, or the dip he was extracting with a pate knife, he barely lifted his gaze from the lighter in his hand.

She found it interesting that along with Hugo and Jed, Phoenix had joined their small club of those who had seen a ghost. She knew Hugo had only told herself and his father about the ghost he had seen, so she would never bring it up unless he did. And she had never admitted to anyone that she too had a ghost in her sights. So what did it say about Phoneix, that he was so willing to share his story with such a large group? He knew very few of them, so had no real understanding of whether they would take him seriously or not. Did that mean Phoenix didn't care what people thought? Was he so comfortable in himself that he would share a ghost story with a group of strangers, no matter the reaction? Or was it just that a few beers brought him out of his shell, and tomorrow he would be the reserved Phoenix Jones had seen so far?

The confidence Jones had that Phoenix could easily be the arsonist was starting to wobble. Why would someone like that feel the need to light fires? It seems his life was interesting and dramatic enough as it was. He didn't seem the type that needed to create the drama and place himself in the centre of it. Yet, what if he had experienced these few moments of drama, like the sight of a ghost and the validation that it was true, and missed the high he got from these times in his life? What if he was continuously seeking more and ever-increasing high-stakes events in his life? Did this new information make him more or less likely to be a suspect?

It was at this moment that Quinn entered The Memory Bank, quickly slamming the door shut before leaning on it and breathing heavily, pulling her t-shirt down from off her face.

"Quinn!" Jones leapt up. "Are you ok?"

Quinn didn't say anything for a minute or so, taking time to catch her breath.

"Do you think we should call an ambulance?" Wren had followed Jones to Quinn's side.

"I'm...ok," Quinn breathed out. "I just...ran...here."

Autumn flew over next to Jones, peering at Quinn.

"Ran? Why?" asked Jones.

"I'm just so sick of the smoke and the heat. It's too much, it's all too much."

Jones looked at Wren. "Water I think," she said. "And a damp cloth for her face." Wren nodded and raced off, whilst Jones guided Quinn to a nearby chair.

Quinn landed heavily, and then bent over her knees, elbows resting, head and hands dangling.

"Just take some long, slow breaths," Jones said to Quinn.

Wren returned with a large glass of water and a wet hand towel from the bathroom. Quinn gulped down the water, and then returned to her position with her head down. Wren placed the cool towel on the back of her neck.

"I'm a bit worried about her," said Jones.

Wren nodded. "I know, but give her a few minutes. If she doesn't seem to pull herself together, then I agree, we might need an ambulance. I just think it could be tricky for them to get into Lilly Pilly Creek.

"Oh gosh, yes you're right," said Jones. "Maybe we should call them anyway, in case it takes them a while to get here."

"I'm fine, I'm fine," said Quinn. She had lifted her head and was certainly looking a little better.

"Have you been out in this all day?" Jones asked.

Quinn nodded. "Of course," said said. "I have to get the story."

"Not by risking your own life!" Jones was crouched down in front of Quinn.

"I know, I know," Quinn shook her head and put her head in her hands.

"You said you ran here? Why?"

"They've blocked the road," she said. "They wouldn't let me through."

"What! So you just got out of your car and ran all the way here?"

"Bloody hell," said Hugo, who had come over to see what all the fuss was about.

"Well, where was I supposed to go?"

"I don't know," said Jones. "Back to Adelaide perhaps. Where it's safe!" She knew she sounded sarcastic, but she truly couldn't believe what she was hearing.

Quinn managed a slight chuckle before beginning to cough. Jones looked at Hugo, alarmed, whilst Wren bent down, rubbing Quinn's back and encouraging her to breathe.

"Quinn, I think we should call an ambulance," said Wren. "You could have smoke inhalation or heat stroke."

"Or both," said Hugo. "I'd drive you, but it sounds like they're not letting anyone in or out."

Quinn went to reply but this just made her coughing worse.

"That's it," said Jones. "I'm calling an ambulance." She pulled out her phone whilst striding away from the group, searching for a quiet spot, Autumn following her.

"Ambulance," Jones said into the phone, before waiting a few moments for someone to answer. "Hello, yes, The Memory Bank, Main Street, Lilly Pilly Creek.......we have a journalist who has been out reporting on the fires and we think she may be suffering smoke inhalation or heat stroke......yes, she's conscious.....yes she is breathing but currently having a coughing fit.....yes, inside, sitting on a chair......" Jones made her way back over to Quinn, Wren and Hugo. "Ok, we need to keep her sitting up. Wren, unbutton the top of her shirt. Quinn, take long, slow breaths. Oh, she shouldn't be drinking anything. She has had water. Ok, ok. We need to keep her awake. Ok, thanks."

Jones stayed on the phone with the dispatcher. "Yes, I imagine it is busy out there and hard to access," she was saying. "It's ok Quinn, they're on their way, just take deep breaths."

Jones was glad she had decided to call. Although Quinn's coughing seemed to be easing up, she certainly appeared to be going downhill. She kept her head down and was only responding with nods or shakes of her head. It felt like hours before the paramedics arrived. Autumn was poking her head through the wall at regular intervals and even flew up above The Memory Bank a few times.

"I can hear them," she finally called. Jones smiled but resisted the urge to say anything until she too could hear the sirens.

"Oh they're nearly here," Jones said to the dispatcher and everyone in the room as soon as she heard the faint peel of the ambulance. "Hugo, can you be ready at the door?"

Hugo nodded and stood by the door, waiting until he heard the loud sirens stop out the front. He didn't want to let too much smoke in, so waited a few moments, before opening the door. Within seconds two paramedics in their green uniforms were inside, and Hugo promptly closed the door against the heat and smoke.

"Thank you, they're here. Thank you so much," said Jones as she ended her phone call.

Hugo, Jones and Wren stood back. Jones glanced around the room to see everyone else was silent, watching from their chairs. She had almost forgotten how many people were taking refuge in The Memory Bank.

The paramedics placed an oxygen mask on Quinn and then checked her temperature before cracking open some cool packs and placing them on her body. One of the paramedics left and brought in the stretcher before they got Quinn laid down on top.

"Will anyone be coming with her?"

Jones glanced around. She knew she should probably offer, but she had a crowd at The Memory Bank, and she didn't feel she could leave them alone. She quickly glanced at Hugo who stepped up. "We don't know her that well, but Jones can ring her work and ask them to get in touch with her family. Is that ok?"

The paramedics nodded, finished packing up, and wheeled Quinn out to the ambulance. They didn't seem phased at all that Quinn would be travelling to the hospital alone.

The room was silent for a few moments after Quinn had been taken away. Drinks were sipped and cheese was eaten. Jones pulled out her phone for any updates on the fire. From what she could tell, it didn't appear to be on their doorstep, but she knew that didn't mean they weren't still in danger. All they could do was sit tight, and hope The Memory Bank kept them safe. After seeing Quinn so affected, she began to worry that The Bank wasn't quite the fortress she had believed it to be.

CHAPTER 21

"Jones!" It was Autumn calling from the book stacks. Jones wasn't quite sure what excuse she would give to anyone asking what she was doing, but she decided to just slowly wander over there, giving the impression she was thinking. Fortunately, quiet discussions were again happening within the group, so she hoped they wouldn't notice her talking to Autumn under her breath.

"Poor Quinn," said Autumn. "Do you think she'll be ok?"

"Gosh, I hope so," said Jones. "She looked awful. I wonder if she got her story in before she collapsed?"

"Her story?" asked Autumn, her mouth agape. "You're worried about her story?"

"Oh no, not like that," Jones said. "I just know what Quinn's like. She'll be devastated if all her efforts today were for nothing if her story doesn't go to print."

"Is it really that important?" Autumn asked, frowning.

"To a journalist, yes it is," said Jones. "She's been out there all day in horrible conditions, and if it doesn't go to print for tomorrow's edition, it'll be old news. Something else is bound to happen tomorrow that trumps today's story."

"That's a bit cutthroat, isn't it?"

"That's the newspaper game, I'm afraid. Tomorrow's fish and chip paper," said Jones. "I'm sure she would have been sending back clips and blurbs throughout the day, so no doubt she'll get some coverage. But I'm sure she would have been preparing a full story."

"To try and get higher than page five," said Autumn, with a grin.

"Exactly!" said Jones.

"You miss it, don't you?" said Autumn.

"What?"

"The newspaper game. Chasing the story. That's why you're being so supportive of Quinn."

"Well, of course, I miss it," said Jones. "But that's ok. We all miss things. And I'd like to think I'd be supportive of Quinn no matter what."

"Yes I know you would be," said Autumn. "That's not what I meant. But do you wish you were out there with her?"

"To be honest, after seeing her just now," Jones shook her head. "No, I don't really."

"But what Quinn did was a bit irresponsible, wouldn't you say?"

"Very irresponsible," said Jones. "I can't quite work out what got into her."

"The story, of course," said Autumn. "She didn't want to miss the story, and I guess going back to Adelaide would mean she was out of the danger zone."

Jones nodded.

"What about Phoenix's story," continued Autumn. "I just don't know what to make of that guy?"

"And a ghost story of all things!" said Jones. "It's like ghosts follow me wherever I go." Jones couldn't help but wink at Autumn who laughed, her head thrown back.

"I still say we keep an eye on him," said Autumn. "There's

something odd about him, and he doesn't let go of that lighter."

"Speaking of his lighter," said Jones. "Have you managed to see what's engraved on it?"

"Yes!" said Autumn. "I did actually. It says 'Who Dares Wins'."

"Interesting," said Jones, pulling out her phone. "Ah, here it is. It's the SASR motto."

"So it's not relevant?" asked Autumn.

Jones shook her head. "It doesn't seem so. A personal motto perhaps?"

Autumn went to float away but Jones called her back. "Wait!"

Autumn twirled back to Jones. "What is it?"

"I just want you to be careful around Phoenix," said Jones.

"Why?"

"What if he can see you? If he's seen one ghost, who's to say he can't see you?"

"Nah, I doubt it," said Autumn, shrugging.

"Oh, you don't? How are you so confident?"

"Didn't you say Hugo has seen a ghost before? He can't see me. And I don't think that wine guy could see me, could he?"

"Jed? Who knows? But what if they can and they're *really* good at hiding it."

Autumn tilted her head and pursed her lips. "Really? Nope, I don't think so. I don't think anyone else has ever seen me, other than you."

"But they've heard you," said Jones.

"They have? Who?"

"Atlas and Plum," said Jones. "I'm sure they've both sensed you. Just be careful. Your energy could be growing and neither of us knows how it works. Maybe that makes it more likely someone is going to find out about you."

"I'll be careful," said Autumn. "I promise." With that, she flew to hover by Phoenix.

Jones wandered over to grab herself some more cheese and then sat next to Hugo, who took her hand. He squeezed it and looked at her with a slight smile. She felt her phone buzz in her hand.

Sybil had messaged to say she had heard the fire was under control, and that Lilly Pilly Creek wasn't under threat.

"Oh, thank goodness," Jones said aloud. All eyes immediately went to her and she quickly explained.

'What a relief,' said Prue. "Does that mean I can head back to the office?"

"Just wait," said Wren who was looking at her phone. "The news isn't up on the CFS website. No doubt Sybil has heard it through her grapevine. I'm sure it's accurate, it's just not official yet. So just stay here where it's safe for now."

Prue sighed but agreed, and helped herself to some more of the food in front of her.

"Bonus information," said Jones, as another message beeped on her phone. "Sybil is handing out free coffees and milkshakes to all the firies!"

There was a small round of applause from the group, appreciating Sybil's generosity.

"She's a good egg, that Sybil," said Rusty.

"Don't go getting any ideas, Rusty!" Hugo cautioned.

"Ha, ha! Although…." he winked at the group, before taking a sip of his beer.

"Well, I won't tell you that she's just parked herself outside," said Jones.

"I didn't hear a thing," Rusty joked.

Jones had to admit, she wasn't sure what she thought about Rusty having a soft spot for Sybil if it was more than just in jest. But who was she to stand in the way of potential love?

She messaged Sybil, suggesting she come inside the Bank. But she declined. She told her the smoke wasn't too bad anymore, and the air conditioning and fan she had going in the van was helping.

The group continued eating, drinking and chatting. Jones found herself unable to sit still, so she wandered around The Memory Bank, tidying the already tidy space, and peering out the window for any signs the atmosphere was changing outside. Autumn let her know she was going out to take a look, and Jones had to admit she was glad to have a ghost available to venture out into the smoke and stifling temperatures, completely unaffected.

Jones's thoughts turned to Atlas. She was relieved that Christopher hadn't pursued him any further. It would be ridiculous of course, and it made sense that he wasn't a serious suspect. It did frustrate her that Atlas had to go through questioning, just because he was the newest member of the crew. He may decide to quit, and if he did, Jones knew they would be missing an exceptional volunteer firefighter.

Hugo walked up and put his arm around her waist. "It's great news they have the fire under control."

"It sure is," said Jones, leaning her head into his shoulder. "It's quite exhausting, sitting around all day, waiting."

Hugo smiled. "That's true," he said. "And now I have to decide if I'm going to reopen the bar. There might be a few hungry and thirsty firefighters out there."

"It's up to you Hugo," said Jones. "Everyone will understand if you stay closed. Would you be able to get staff back anyway?"

"I'm not sure," he shrugged. "I'll wait a bit longer. Just because we have the word from Sybil, doesn't mean they'll even be letting people back into Lilly Pilly Creek."

"Oh yes," said Jones. "That's true. Best to wait, right here with me." She smiled and hugged him, whilst he kissed the top of her head.

She couldn't deny it had been nice spending the afternoon with Hugo, without the distraction of Memory Bank customers or Hugo having to race back and forth to the bar. Although they hadn't really had time to themselves, just being in each other's company, she realised, happened far less than she would like.

As Jones turned to face Hugo, taking his hands in hers, and looking up into his eyes, The Memory Bank door was opened.

CHAPTER 22

There, standing in their yellow and orange CFS uniforms were Atlas, and his boss, Candace, each carrying one of Sybil's free milkshakes.

"Atlas!" called out Jones, running over to him. "But you're in your uniform?" She was confused, but then realised, as soon as Christopher had given him the all-clear, he had headed straight back out to the fire.

At that moment Autumn slid through the front door. Jones presumed she had spotted them both from whatever vantage point she had been at.

"He sure is," said Candace, pulling the door closed. "And he did an amazing job."

Jones looked at the woman standing next to Atlas. At that moment she was very tempted to give her a piece of her mind. How dare she accuse Atlas of arson one day and then tell them all what they already knew, that yes, Atlas was amazing.

"Well, of course he did," said Jones, slapping his arm. "Come on Atlas, come over and grab some food."

Jones knew it was obvious she was ignoring Candace, and she didn't care one bit. It was the least she could do.

Walking him over, Jones whispered, "Atlas, are you sure you're ok? I mean, after this morning and everything?"

Atlas nodded. "Of course I am. And thank you. I know you were involved in getting Wren there."

"I didn't do a thing," said Jones. "But Christopher, was he ok? He wasn't too tough on you?"

"Not at all," said Atlas. "Professional like always. Didn't want to risk getting too personal in front of other people. And Wren kept things short and to the point of course."

"Good, as she should. Who else was there?"

"A woman from Adelaide. A fire investigator, but she didn't say much. Just stared at me the whole time with a frown on her face.

Jones smiled. "But you went back out to the fire? After everything?"

"Of course," said Atlas. "I've got nothing to hide. Why shouldn't I be out here?"

"Yes, you're right," said Jones. "Although I'd much rather you were safe here at The Memory Bank."

Atlas laughed, and Jones left him to fill up on the platter that never seemed to diminish, no matter how much they all consumed.

Jones glanced around and was somewhat surprised to see Wren talking to Candace. She hoped it was with an investigative mindset and not simple chit-chat. Jones despite knowing nothing else about this woman, was utterly unimpressed with her at this stage.

"That woman," said Autumn, her eyes boring a hole into Candace Chadwick.

"What are you doing? Get over there and listen," Jones hissed.

Hugo was talking with Atlas, and Jones watched as he properly introduced him to his three friends. A lot of handshaking all round, and then it appeared the fellas had a lot of questions for the firefighter now in their midst. Jones smiled as she watched Atlas sit down and animatedly describe his day.

She noticed Prue must have snuck out, eager to get back to the office before official word came in. Jones would never understand that woman, but she supposed she couldn't knock her work ethic.

It was then Jones remembered Quinn, and that she hadn't rung The Advertiser. Quickly pulling out her phone, she rang the switchboard and asked for Quinn's editor, Jock Mitchell.

"Jock, it's Jones Eldershaw."

"Jones! It's been a while! How are you? Are you ringing to tell me you're headed back?"

"Unfortunately no," said Jones.

"Unfortunately?"

"Unfortunately in the face of what I'm ringing you about."

"Oh? What is it?"

"It's Quinn McCoy."

"Quinn? What's happened?"

"Well, she's just gone to hospital by ambulance."

"She has? Why? Where are you?"

"I'm in Lilly Pilly Creek. Where the fires are that she's been reporting on. I think she's headed to Mount Barker. They're worried she has smoke inhalation or heat exhaustion."

"Crikey," he said. "What's she doing out there?"

"She's out on a story, isn't she?"

"Yep, yep, that's right," said Jock.

Jones frowned. "Well, I thought you'd need to know. You'd have her emergency contacts. I think they took her to the Mount Barker

Hospital. There's no one with her at the moment."

"Right, right, yep, I'll get onto that straight away. Thanks for letting me know, Jones."

"No problems," said Jones. "I hope she's ok."

"Thanks," said Jock. "And Jones?"

"Yes, Jock?"

"You know you're welcome back any time. We're crying out for decent reporters!"

Jones couldn't help but smile. "Thanks, Jock, I'll let you know when I'm back in the building."

She hung up, feeling a little guilty that she had taken so long to ring him. Quinn had slipped her mind so quickly.

There was a loud banging on the front door. Jones wondered why they didn't just walk in, but she went over and opened it anyway.

"Christopher?" She was surprised to see the Police Sergeant standing there, next to him another uniformed officer.

"Miss Eldershaw," said Christopher. "Is Atlas here?"

"He is," said Jones. "But I thought that was all sorted?"

Christopher frowned at her, and she saw his eyes quickly dart to the woman at his side. Jones got it. He couldn't say anything with the city cop listening.

"Could you please let him know I need to speak to him," he said. "We'll wait out here."

"Sure," Jones nodded, appreciating at least that Christopher was trying to be discreet. But she couldn't believe it. They surely didn't still think Atlas had anything to do with yesterday's fire?

Jones walked up to Atlas and gently grabbed his arm. He turned, and she whispered in his ear. "Christopher is outside. He needs to speak to you." She watched as his eyes bulged, and then he let his chin drop to his chest. "It'll be ok Atlas. Go and talk to Wren before you walk outside." She patted him on the back. "Deep breath. Off you go."

She watched as Atlas pulled Wren to one side. Wren frowned, and then gripped Atlas's upper arms, obviously giving him a pep talk. As they walked out the door, Jones wondered what had changed in the last few hours.

Then she realised. Today's fire must have been deliberately lit also.

Her eyes whipped around the room, desperately searching for her sister, but she was nowhere to be seen. Jones was ashamed to admit it, but she hoped Autumn had ignored their previous agreement and was currently eavesdropping on Atlas, Wren and the police.

She made her way over to Hugo who was standing with Candace and his friends. They were commenting on the sudden exit of Wren and Atlas. Jones glanced at Hugo and shook her head. She didn't want him to say anything about Atlas, and it appeared that Candace in her role as Crew Captain, to give her credit, was acting professional.

"Probably nothing to do with the fire," said Candace. "I have a debrief scheduled with the big wigs this evening, so there won't be any more information until then."

Jones nodded in Candace's direction. Jones knew it wasn't true, and assumed Candace knew that too. It seemed despite evidence otherwise, that she was perhaps looking out for Atlas.

"A tough day today, I imagine," Jones said to Candace. She wanted to extend her at least half an olive branch. Perhaps she hadn't thrown Atlas under the bus like they thought. Or, she was very good at hiding her true feelings, at playing the part.

"Very," said Candace. "One of the toughest days I've been a part of. The late wind change threw everyone and we were scrambling for a bit. Luckily everything went our way in the end."

"Any idea what started it?" asked Chappy.

Jones noticed Candace pause before framing her response. "That is still under investigation," she said. "Can be tricky. Still a lot going on at the fire ground. I imagine we'll know soon enough." Candace slurped the last of her milkshake. "Opening the bar tonight, Hugo?" she asked.

"I was waiting until the roads opened again," said Hugo. "But doesn't look like that's happening any time soon." He indicated a notice he was reading on his phone.

"Ok, well, I might head home for a proper shower then, before my meeting. Thanks for the feed!" Candace nodded at the group and made her way out.

Jones watched her walk away, and Hugo came to stand beside her.

"I can't work that woman out," said Jones. "What do you think of her?"

"Seems nice enough. Professional."

"Do you think *she* could have started the fires?"

"Fires?" asked Hugo, looking at Jones. "You mean today was arson too?"

"You saw Wren and Atlas leave," said Jones.

"Yeah, what was that all about?"

"Christopher and the city cop wanted to speak to Atlas."

"What? Again? I thought that was all sorted?"

Jones looked up sadly at Hugo. "So did I. But it seems someone has their sights set on Atlas."

"That's ridiculous! Not a chance Atlas has anything to do with it."

"That's what I think too," said Jones. "And I'm wondering whether Candace, or someone else," she didn't say Phoenix, but she was thinking it. "If they're the real suspects and they've managed to avoid detection because for some reason the police think Atlas is the culprit."

"You think Candace has pointed the finger at Atlas to avoid them looking at her?"

"Makes sense, doesn't it?"

"Bloody hell," said Hugo.

CHAPTER 23

With the roads blocked, Jones invited Hugo and the three blokes to stay at her place. Even though they needed the bed, Jones couldn't bring herself to let anyone sleep in Autumn's room.

Rusty won rock paper scissors and took the bed Quinn had been sleeping in. He even happily changed the sheets. Hugo quietly explained to Phoenix and Chappy why Autumn's bedroom was off-limits, and they settled themselves on the lounges.

Hugo of course, shared a bed with Jones. They hadn't spent many nights together, taking things slowly. But Hugo had stayed over a few times, and she had been to his tiny house as well. They were beginning to feel comfortable with each other, although Jones had to admit it felt a little strange to be hosting Hugo's friends in her house. As though they were playing husband and wife long before they were ready. Fortunately, Hugo left Jones to all the hosting and just pitched in to help with finding towels for everyone at Jones's direction, whilst she put some eggs, bacon and tomatoes on the barbeque She even found some fritz to throw on. Despite all the snacking they had done that afternoon, by the evening everyone was ready for something more substantial to eat, and a fry-up was the best Jones could manage.

As the men put themselves through the showers, fortunately having their bags of clothes with them, Hugo and Jones stood together outside, drinking a glass of white wine, as Jones manned the barbie. The air was still heavy with smoke, and although it was a relief that the wind had died down, it did mean the evening was very warm.

There would be no cooling breeze tonight, with another scorcher forecast for tomorrow.

"Will Wren let you know what's happening?" Hugo asked.

"I have no idea," said Jones. "She is very professional. She won't speak out of turn when it comes to client confidentiality. But she may give me a hint as to how worried we should be."

Jones wanted to mention that rather than relying on Wren, she was relying on her sister to have the inside word. She hadn't seen Autumn since Atlas and Wren left. She presumed she had stayed with them. Jones guessed the 'interview' would have finished long ago, but Autumn would need to return to The Memory Bank to regain her energy.

"It's just astounding that the cops still think Atlas had something to do with it?"

"Well, I've been thinking about that," said Jones, pausing with her tongs in the air.

"Oh yes?" said Hugo, sipping his wine.

"Maybe they don't think Atlas has anything to do with it," she explained. "Maybe they think he has information about the suspect."

"About Candace Chadwick, you mean?"

Jones glanced at Hugo. "A possibility, don't you think?"

Hugo paused, staring out to the hazy sky where the sun had almost set over the ranges.

"It does," he said. "Atlas being new means he could be one of the most unbiased on the crew. And we know he has an excellent attention to detail. Maybe this is all a bit of a ruse to draw out the real firebug."

Hugo tilted his glass towards Jones, acknowledging her clever thoughts.

"I think so too," said Jones, flipping the bacon before reaching for her wine. "At least, I hope so."

The couple stood at the barbie, staring as the food sizzled and popped. The exhaustion was starting to creep in, even though Jones couldn't explain it. They hadn't done much at all that day, besides worrying. Being on edge for twelve hours did take it out of you. She could only imagine how the CFS fireys were feeling.

Chappy poked his head out the door. "Jones, is this your phone?" The phone in his hand was indeed Jones's and it was buzzing, a number she didn't know was on the screen. She took it and answered.

"Is that Jones?"

"This is Jones," she replied, not recognising the man's voice.

"Oh thank goodness," the voice said. "This is Dave Hemming, Atlas's dad. We didn't know who else to call. We're on holiday in Robe. But we've just had a call from Atlas."

"You have?" Jones frowned. "I know he was speaking to the police but is everything ok."

"No I'm afraid it's not," said Mr Hemming. "He's been arrested."

"What!" Jones couldn't believe what she was hearing. She almost dropped her phone, her hand instinctively reaching for her throat. "That's impossible. Surely not!"

"Not from what Atlas told me," said Mr Hemming. Jones could hear a woman sobbing in the background. "We're packing up straight away, but he must be so scared. Jones, do you think you can see if you can do anything?"

"Of course, of course," said Jones. "I know Wren was with him. But I'll head straight down there."

"Can you hurry," he said. "I think they're taking him to Mount Barker Police Station tonight."

"Seriously! For goodness sake. Leave it with me," said Jones. "I'll keep in touch."

Jones hung up and turned to Hugo. "They've arrested Atlas. Can you believe it!"

"No!" said Hugo. "What does that mean exactly?"

"I have no idea," said Jones. "I'm heading straight to the police station now. I want to catch them before they transfer him."

"Do you want me to come?" Hugo asked.

Jones shook her head. "No, look can you just hold the fort here? Feed the fellas and make sure they're ok. I'm sure I won't be allowed to stay long."

Hugo took the tongs from Jones's hands before hugging her. "It will be ok," said Hugo. "I'm sure of it."

Jones nodded, and then rolled her shoulders back and took a deep breath. "I'm going to keep it together, for Atlas's sake."

Jones grabbed her keys and purse and raced out the door, with barely a glance at the three men who were in her house, making themselves at home in front of the TV.

Racing through the streets in her Mini Cooper, it only took her a couple of minutes to skid to a stop in front of the Station. She was surprised to see Autumn there. Was she waiting for her?

"Autumn! Are you ok?"

"I'm fine," she said. "I have to head straight back to The Memory Bank, but I was waiting for you. I heard Atlas tell his Dad to call you, so I presumed you wouldn't be long."

"What is going on? Why have they arrested Atlas?"

"They're saying the tyre marks of the vehicle near the crime scenes match his tyres."

"Crime scenes plural? So today's fire *was* deliberately lit?"

"Yes, exactly," said Autumn. "They can only hold him for up to eight hours from what I hear. So they're taking him to Mount Barker, but it sounds like, if they don't charge him, he'll be released late tonight."

"Well of course they can't charge him! There'll be others with the same tyre treads."

"Just get in there Jones, before they leave," said Autumn. "I'm heading back to The Memory Bank. Come and see me later if you want. Otherwise, we can talk tomorrow."

Jones desperately wanted to hug her sister but settled with a quick wave before walking into the station. It was late, and she was surprised the front door wasn't locked. Hurriedly she pressed the bell on the counter multiple times. She couldn't hear the ring, but she presumed it was working and someone out the back would hear it.

Leaning on the counter, she fruitlessly attempted to push herself up so she could better peer through the striped mirror glass on the inner door. Fortunately, in under a minute, the door opened and out walked Christopher.

"What the hell is going on!" Jones burst. Christopher raised one eyebrow. She immediately regretted it. "Sorry, sorry Christopher. I'll start again. How is Atlas? What can I do?"

"That's ok," said Christopher. "I understand everyone is a bit stressed at the moment. I don't think there is anything you *can* do.'

"But why Christopher? You surely don't believe Atlas has done anything?"

"Jones, you know I can't talk about this," he said. "But they are taking him to Mount Barker because they feel they will have, how can I put it, better luck getting information." Christopher was staring at Jones, and she knew she was supposed to read something into what he was saying. That they didn't trust Christopher was unbiased in this situation and needed to separate him from Atlas, is how Jones interpreted his intense look.

Jones nodded and rolled her yes. "Of course they do," said Jones. "Can I see him?"

Christopher shook his head. "No, he has Wren in there with him, and no one else can be with him at the moment. He's spoken to his parents, and that's all I can allow at this stage.

"And can they just keep him there indefinitely?"

"No they can't,' said Christopher. "If they don't charge him with anything, he will likely get released very early this morning." Christopher glanced at this watch. "Sometime around three."

"Three! Gosh! And I don't suppose they'll let him sleep," said Jones.

"He might get a cat nap if he can fall asleep," said Christopher.

"Will Wren be with him the whole time?" she asked.

Christopher nodded. "I believe that is the plan. She will have to take her own car, so I suppose she can drive him home too."

"I'll go with her," said Jones. "I'll go there and I'll wait."

"It may be better if you get some sleep," he suggested. "You might be more help tomorrow."

Jones groaned. She had no idea what to do. She had promised his parents she would do anything she could to help. She knew they would be at the police station waiting if they could be. But what was the most sensible thing to do?

"Will Wren come out this way? Before they leave?"

"I'll let her know you're here if you like?"

"Yes, please," said Jones. "And Christopher?"

"Yes?"

"I'm sorry for my outburst before," Jones apologised. "I know you would be doing everything you can, and being professional. Thank you."

Christopher nodded, before returning to the back of the station.

CHAPTER 24

Jones managed to catch Wren on the way out.

"It's awful Jones," said Wren. "But from what I've heard, the only thing they have is the car tyres, and I'm not even convinced they are a perfect match. It's a stretch. But Atlas is going to have to go through the motions for now. He just has to keep his head."

"It's not fair!" said Jones. "How can they treat him this way?"

"This is policing, unfortunately," said Wren. "But I'm doing everything I can."

"I know you are Wren, thank you."

Wren asked her to call Atlas's parents and tell them to meet her at Mount Barker. It seemed if they were already in the car driving from Robe, they should be only about four hours away. They would be able to take Atlas home themselves. Wren confirmed what Christopher had said. There was no point in Jones sitting at the station. They wouldn't let her speak to Atlas and there was nothing she could do.

"And if he gets charged, well he won't be going anywhere anyway," Wren.

"Oh Wren, you won't let that happen, will you?"

"I'm doing everything I can," said Wren. "But I'm going to have to contact one of my colleagues who has experience in these types of cases because I'm going to be out of my depth if this goes any further."

"Thanks, Wren," said Jones. "Thank you for helping Atlas."

"Of course," said Wren. "Now I'd better get going so I'm there when they start to interview him again."

They hugged each other before Wren got in her car. Poor Wren would be exhausted tomorrow too.

Jones stood outside the police station, watching the lights of Wren's car disappear. The smoky air lay heavy on her shoulders, as though she had been enveloped by a weighted blanket. She had no ability to help Atlas, and everything seemed to be spiralling out of control. She knew Atlas would be depending on her. He would be expecting her to investigate. To find the real culprit and save him. But who? Candace? Phoenix? Was there anyone else? Perhaps she needed to cast a wider net. It could be almost anyone. So, why were the police so fixated on a brand-new CFS volunteer? Just because arsonists were often connected to the fire service, didn't mean they were in this case. Should she say something to Christopher? Make her suspicions known? Except that's exactly what they were, suspicions. She had no evidence whatsoever.

The only thing Jones could think of to do was to go and talk with her sister. The Eldershaw Sisters Detective Agency needed to get serious about this case, their most important one yet. Although only five minutes down the road, Jones got back in her car, wanting to avoid breathing in as much smoke as possible. She hoped tomorrow the ash in the air would start to dissipate.

"Autumn!" Jones called as she made her way into The Memory Bank. "Autumn!"

Jones spun in the middle of the Bank's main room, searching for where her sister would appear from. On her third spin, she saw her sister zoom down through the ceiling.

"Jones! What's wrong?"

"So much," said Jones, shaking her head. "But where were you?"

"Sitting on the roof," said Autumn.

"Do you do that a lot?"

Autumn nodded. "It's nice to watch the stars. Although they're hard to see tonight. All I can see is spots of flame scattered over the hills."

"What, the fire's still burning?"

"All over," said Autumn. "But I think it's just trees smouldering, not a full blaze. I imagine there are a lot of CFS out there tonight, keeping an eye on things for us."

"Well, there's one member of the CFS who most certainly isn't out there."

"Oh?" Autumn frowned.

"Atlas has been arrested," said Jones.

"What!" said Autumn. "But I thought he had been cleared?"

Jones sighed and made her way over to a table, slumping down in a chair. "They've got it in for him," said Jones, noticing her voice wobble.

"Who's got it in for him?"

"Oh, those city police," said Jones. "They're taking him to Mount Barker, to interrogate him. And there's nothing Christopher or Wren can do!"

"They can't be serious!" said Autumn. "Why aren't they out there trying to find the real arsonist? Of course, it isn't Atlas. How can they be so stupid?"

Jones groaned, but couldn't form any words. Autumn was right. How could the police be so stupid? Though she supposed that was easy for them to say. They knew Atlas. Knew he would never deliberately cause anyone harm. But those city detectives didn't know him from a bar of soap. They thought they had the right person, and they weren't going to let him slip out of their fingers.

"It's up to us Autumn," said Jones. "We have to find out who this arsonist is before it's too late."

"But who?" Autumn cried. "Who is it? The only suspect we have is Phoenix. Do we think it could be him?"

"Well, he's certainly a better suspect than Atlas!"

"Have you spoken to Hugo about this?" asked Autumn.

"Of course, I haven't," said Jones, slightly more grumpily than she meant. "No, and I don't think I can. Especially when the only evidence we have is a moody man holding a cigarette lighter."

"Ah yeah, a cigarette lighter that is perfect for, you know, lighting fires!"

Jones shook her head. "I know, I know," she said. "But it's a little weak. We need more. And we can't behave like the police. We can't narrow our focus on one person. We need to consider all possible culprits."

"Like who?" Autumn asked.

"I don't know," Jones moaned, dropping her head into her hands.

"Ok, ok," said Autumn. "Look, let's stop and think about this logically. Who benefits from the arson? The fires?"

Jones didn't respond for a while, her head remaining in her hands.

She did her best to think, but she was tired and frustrated and couldn't seem to get her brain to work.

"Could they be covering up another crime?" asked Autumn. "Maybe the arson is just a front for something else?"

Jones slowly lifted her head and looked at her sister. That was a really good point. Maybe they weren't looking for an arsonist. Maybe they were looking for another type of criminal!

"Murder? Vandalism? Insurance fraud?" Jones threw out suggestions as she stood and began pacing the Bank.

"Yes! Yes!" said Autumn as she began to fly around the room. "I mean, all of this is arson, but it gives a completely different motive which means-"

"A completely different type of criminal!"

The sisters looked at each other beaming. They *were* so much better together.

"So, who could this be?" asked Jones, moving behind the counter, and grabbing her pen and notebook.

"The farmer, what was his name?"

"Rhys! Rhys...Rhys...Bauer!"

"Yes! Put him at the top of the list," said Autumn. "And I guess we need to find out where this fire started today. See if it's connected to him, or if there's another culprit."

"Oh right, that's good," said Jones, writing 'unknown property owner' with a question mark. "Which brings us to something we haven't considered."

"What's that?"

"What if the two fires were started by two different people?"

"You think there could be two firebugs out there? Doesn't that seem unlikely?"

"Maybe," said Jones, shrugging. "But maybe we have a copycat. Maybe someone heard about the arson and realised they could start a fire to, cover up their own crime, and it could all point back to the first arsonist?"

Autumn nodded. "You're right! That could totally be the case. I wonder if the police know of anything that links the two crimes? Or if they are two completely different cases? I wonder how we might find that out?"

"Wren did mention something," said Jones

"Did she?"

"Yes," she said, sighing. "The tyre tracks. There are tyre tracks at the two ignition points, which they are saying match Atlas's car."

"Which of course they don't," said Autumn.

"No," said Jones. "But the police say they match. I don't know. Wren didn't think they had a match for Atlas's car. So maybe they're wrong about the two sets matching?"

"Well, we're going to have to find out. But how?"

Jones rolled her eyes. "You know exactly how we're going to find that out!"

"Why such a sarcastic tone? How?" asked Autumn.

"You're going to read the file notes, of course!"

"What! While you're sweet talking Christopher?"

"Oh shut up!" But Jones was grinning. She knew it was wrong, but if she had to sweet talk Christopher to save Atlas, then she realised she wasn't above that kind of behaviour.

"If we get the opportunity," said Jones. "I suppose we should take it. I just don't see how that can happen."

"You know I will," said Autumn with a wink.

"Ok, let's focus," said Jones. "We can come up with all the motives we want, but we need to put some more names on this list."

"Well, you have to add Phoenix," said Autumn. "We at least have to investigate him. Just because I get a really weird vibe from him."

"Ok, I'll put Phoenix on here," said Jones. "But we cannot let Hugo see this list."

"Of course," said Autumn. "Now, who else? Who else would benefit from the fires?"

"I still think we need to put Candace on the list," said Jones. "She could be framing Atlas. She gets to not only save the community but nail the arsonist. Seems that wouldn't harm her career."

"Ok, put her down," said Autumn. "We don't know much about her, although when she was in the Bank earlier, she seemed happy Atlas was back."

"That could've just been a front," said Jones. "But I agree, she did protect him."

"Yes, you're right," said Autumn. "Is there anyone else who benefits from all of this?"

The two thought, Jones tapping her pen against her lips, and Autumn spinning slowly underneath the chandelier.

"Ok, now, what I'm about to say next may sound crazy," said

Autumn. "But hear me out."

"Sure," said Jones. "I'm listening."

"Well, you know who else benefits from all of this?"

"Who?"

"The city detectives.""You think these city detectives may have caused the fires?"

"And then pinned in on Atlas? Absolutely!" said Autumn. "Perhaps they're trying to get a promotion or big-note themselves. What better way than to catch an arsonist!"

"But there is no way we are going to be able to accuse them," said Jones.

"Not without irrefutable evidence," said Autumn.

"That's going to be tough," said Jones. "But I see what you're thinking. Is there anyone else out there that gets benefit from these fires, that doesn't seem connected?"

"What about people who have to rebuild after the fires? There are fencing, sheds, and houses that will need to be rebuilt. Or maybe properties will need to be sold?"

"Are you talking about Prue?" asked Jones.

Autumn shrugged. "I wouldn't put it past her. To at least give someone else the idea, knowing she was going to reap the rewards later."

"That is abominable!" said Jones.

"That's Prue," said Autumn.

"Ok, I know I've considered her my nemesis in the past, but I don't think she's evil. Do you think she's evil?"

"Honestly, I have no idea," said Autumn. "I just find it so horrifying that anyone would believe Atlas was the culprit, I may be spreading the net too wide."

"I think we need to sleep on it," said Jones. "Or at least I'll sleep on it, and you can go back to the roof."

Autumn smiled. "Yes, I think sleep will do you good. We need to be ready tomorrow to do whatever we can to help Atlas.

Jones wished her sister goodnight and made her way outside of The Memory Bank. She knew their theories were getting more wild and absurd, but they were desperate. If they could throw any doubt on the detective's case against Atlas, that was a good thing, right?

CHAPTER 25

"Eek!"

Jones's eyes flew open.

"What the bloody hell is that?" asked Hugo who was lying next to her.

"I made the front cover!" the voice squealed.

"Quinn," said Jones. Although what she was doing back here Jones couldn't work out. If she'd been released from hospital you think she would have gone home. Jones raised her eyebrows but couldn't help smiling. She was happy for Quinn. She worked hard and deserved the cover story. "Coffee?" she asked Hugo, getting up and putting on her dressing gown.

Jones realised Quinn may not be aware they had a house full of guests and wanted to warn her. But she quickly realised she was too late.

"Argh!"

As Jones opened the bedroom door Quinn ran past her. Jones turned to see Rusty in a pair of boxer shorts, standing in the doorway to the bedroom Quinn had previously occupied.

"Is that how a bloke gets woken up around here?" he asked, rubbing his face.

"Rusty," said Jones. "You've scared Quinn half to death."

"Whaddaya think she did to me! Can only wonder what the other blokes are gonna think."

"Oh, crap!" Jones rushed down the hallway only to find Quinn, eyes wide, staring at the two tattooed men raising their heads from the couches.

"What's got you so chirpy?" Chappy eyeballed Quinn.

Quinn turned her head to face Jones, mouth wide.

"Quinn, meet Chappy and Phoenix."

Quinn let out a huge sigh her face turning a fetching shade of magenta.

"I'm so sorry," said Quinn. "I didn't realise anyone else was here." She turned to Jones. "I thought you'd like to see." Quinn raised her eyebrows and handed Jones the newspaper she had been clutching.

Across the page was the silhouette of a kangaroo, bounding in front of a wall of flames engulfing a stand of gum trees. It was a stunning, powerful photo and across the top read "The Hills in Flames." Quinn's story began on the bottom third of the page. For a journalist, this was quite an achievement.

"Oh Quinn," Jones looked up, smiling. "This is wonderful." Hugo had walked in and she held up the newspaper to show him, before displaying it to the others.

"I can't believe it," she said, appearing somewhat shy. "I didn't really believe I'd get the cover. I thought surely something else would take it."

"You deserve it," said Jones. "You've been working so hard. But how did you get back into Lilly Pilly Creek? You went to the hospital.

"It's amazing what lines you can cross when you're driving a News vehicle," said Quinn, "My boss let me take a work four-wheel drive. Mum came with me so she could drive mine home." She was grinning, a little cheekily, clearly pleased with herself.

"So Jock is happy with you?"

"As happy as he gets, I suppose," said Quinn. "He's sent me to officially cover the story, so I guess he's not angry with me at least."

"What, you weren't on official newspaper business?" Jones asked, moving around behind the kitchen counter to grab a pen and paper. She was going to take everyone's orders before calling in her coffee order to Sybil.

"Well, technically, the last few days I've been freelancing," said Quinn.

"Freelancing? Why do you mean?"

"I took leave and sent the stories in without being asked to," said Quinn. "Thankfully that paid off!"

"Yes that's very lucky," said Jones. "I'm surprised Jock even read your story! He doesn't usually appreciate it when people go about things outside of the normal way."

Quinn laughed. "No, he does not! I'm surprised he even let me get page five yesterday, so I knew I was going to have to impress him. Thank god I got that photo! I sent that to him first and he couldn't resist it."

Jones wrote 'Coffee Order?' at the top of the piece of paper she had and handed it to Rusty with a pen, who was still standing there in his boxers. He nodded and started writing.

"Very clever," said Jones, turning back to see Quinn spreading the newspaper out on the counter. "I have to say that is some photo."

Quinn flipped the page and began reading. Jones stood next to her, reading over her shoulder.

"Arson?" Jones asked. She peered at Quinn. Jones already knew about the arson, but she didn't think the police had released that information.

Quinn didn't take her eyes off the page. "Yep," she said. "Although, I don't think they're a hundred per cent certain. It could have been anything."

"Anything?" said Jones. "Like what?" Jones knew the police were very confident it was arson, but she wondered what they had told Quinn.

"I don't know," said Quinn, continuing to read. "They just said, they were investigating all possibilities, but arson is more newsworthy so I had to include it."

Jones nodded and kept reading. "So this one started on a farm too?" Quinn's story said the fire started near the farm of a woman named Sally Butler.

"That's what I was told," said Quinn. "Only her shearing shed burnt down but the house was fine. And I'm told not a single person was hurt.

"I imagine it's going to be pretty expensive to rebuild a shearing shed," said Jones, her mind flashing back to her conversation with Autumn the previous evening.

"Yeah, but her insurance will cover it," said Quinn.

Her insurance. Could Ms Butler be responsible for burning down her own shearing shed? She was looking forward to speaking to Autumn and adding Sally Butler to their list of suspects.

"What about the other fire?" asked Jones. "Did that farmer lose any property?"

Quinn looked up at Jones, scrunching her eyes, thinking. "Ah, I don't recall. I think there was maybe a worker's cottage that was damaged. I'm not sure. But again, that would be covered by insurance." She went back to reading her own story.

Jones nodded, quickly glancing at Hugo who was sitting on the arm of the couch, wishing she could talk with someone. But with another possible suspect in the room, Phoenix, Jones didn't want to give anyone any ideas. Or reveal that she was investigating. Although by the way Hugo raised his eyebrows and grinned at her, she suspected he was on to her.

"Well, has everyone written down their coffee orders?" Jones took her chance to change the subject. "Quinn, what coffee would you like?" Quinn ordered an extra strong iced coffee, and Jones added her flat white to the bottom, so she wouldn't forget.

Jones picked up her phone and saw there was a text message from Wren. It had come through at four o'clock that morning. Jones felt her stomach drop. In all the hubbub she had completely forgotten to check on Atlas. She dreaded what the message would say.

She walked over to Hugo and stood next to him whilst she read.

Atlas is ok. His parents have taken him home. They haven't charged him. I'll talk to you later.

"Thank goodness," Jones said under her breath, before holding up the message to Hugo. He read it before smiling at Jones and reaching his arm around her waist, squeezing gently.

Jones took a deep breath and refocused.

"Hi Sybil," said Jones into her phone. "I'm hoping you're taking orders this morning?"

"I sure am!" Sybil said. "Flat out here in fact. All the firies are on a shift change."

Jones gave her their order and also added an egg and bacon roll for everyone.

"And no rush Sybil," said Jones. "I'll drive to you in a few moments. I still have to get dressed anyway. Where are you today?"

"Parked right outside the CFS shed actually," said Sybil.

"Smart move!" Jones said before hanging up.

Hugo followed Jones to her bedroom, offering to help collect the order and they got dressed together.

"Quinn will be alright with the three guys, won't she?" asked Jones, choosing a t-shirt from the basket of clean washing on her floor. Today Jones's t-shirt said *'Even the darkest night will end and the sun will rise'* from Les Misérables.

"What are you worried about?" Hugo asked as he pulled his jeans on.

"They won't rib her too much about waking them up, will they?"

"Probably!" Hugo laughed. "I think she can handle herself though."

"Just as long as she doesn't get too enthusiastic about her big cover story," said Jones.

"Don't worry. They'll bring her down a peg or two as required," said Hugo, and they laughed as they made their way out of the house.

Jones got into the front seat of her mini, and Hugo reached in to pull the passenger seat back before he could manoeuvre his way in.

With a click of their seatbelts, Jones reversed out and headed towards Sybil's.

"Still so smoky," Jones said. "And so hot. Here's hoping nothing flares up again today."

Hugo looked out the window, watching the gum tree branches shake and shiver. "All we can hope for is that cool change to come in early. But it's not looking good."

They continued in silence towards Sybil's coffee van. After yesterday's close call, Jones felt sure lighting wouldn't strike twice. But she knew that fires had a mind of their own, and with smouldering trees and stumps no doubt a cause for concern, they couldn't relax at this stage.

Jones was pleased to see there were only a few of the CFS crew still waiting for coffees, with most standing around holding hot and iced coffees, chatting. Their faces were smeared with soot, the top of their overalls pulled off their shoulders and hanging around their waist, cooler in their t-shirts that the whole get up. Jones bet all of them were dying for a shower and a sleep.

"Morning Jones! Hugo!" called Sybil. "Your order will be up soon."

"Thanks, Sybil!"

Jones and Hugo leant against the van in the shade of the awning.

"Are you going to open up today?" Hugo asked Jones.

"Yes, I think so," said Jones. "I mean, I'm not expecting many customers, especially if some of the roads are still closed. But I want to be open, just in case anyone needs a safe place again."

Hugo nodded.

"What about you?" asked Jones.

"I will too," said Hugo. "Thought I might put on a special for the CFS for meals. What do you think?"

Jones took Hugo's hand. "I think that's a great idea!"

Hugo pulled her hand up to his mouth and kissed it.

"Here you go you two," said Sybil. Jones turned her head up to see Sybil handing them both an iced coffee. "On me, while you wait. It's going to take a few minutes to get all the rolls done."

"Oh, thanks, Sybil!" Jones knew she could decline, but the idea of an iced coffee right then was too much to refuse.

"What's the update on the fire?" asked Hugo, turning to lean on Sybil's counter. Jones stepped up next to him.

Sybil glanced around before bringing her head down closer to them. "Definitely arson, again."

"That's awful," said Jones. "Do they know if it's the same person?"

"They're pretty sure it's the same person, but have you heard about-" Sybil stopped talking, looking down at the floor. Jones realised what she was about to say.

"Atlas?" Jones asked tentatively. She had hoped it wasn't public knowledge, but if anyone was going to hear what no one else had, it would be Sybil.

"So you do know," said Sybil. "It's it terrible. It seems like all these guys think he's done it. They haven't said anything to me, but they aren't exactly quiet."

"It's ridiculous," said Jones, frowning, resisting the urge to slam her fist down. "And if this lot are gossiping about it, then what hope does Atlas have?"

"I think he's got a lot of hope," said Sybil. "With you in his corner."

Jones shook her head. "I'm not feeling very helpful. Of course, *we* know it's not Atlas, but who else could it be?" Jones glanced quickly at Hugo, her mind flicking to Phoenix, before returning to Sybil. "Have you heard anything else?'

Sybil shook her head. "Nope," she said. "But I have to say I've only really been serving the firefighters for the last twenty-four hours. I need to hear from some others. Hopefully, everyone will be allowed back in soon, then I'll get the real story."

"If you do hear anything," said Jones. "Anything at all, can you please let me know, immediately? For Atlas?"

Sybil handed Hugo two trays of coffee, before handing Jones bags full of rolls. "Of course, I will," she said.

CHAPTER 26

The group, except for Quinn who was on her way out again, were huddled around Jones's dining table, devouring the egg and bacon sandwiches and their coffee. Quinn had ignored Jones's pleas to stay put, that she had put herself at risk yesterday, and instead waved to Jones as she quickly left the house.

At the table, all talk was on the fires. Hugo of course didn't hesitate to share the rumours that it was arson, but he didn't share that Atlas was the prime suspect. Jones nodded in appreciation.

"Bloody hell," said Chappy. "What type of bloke lights fires? Seriously!"

Jones couldn't help but glance at Phoenix before responding. "Or woman. I have read that women are often arsonists as well." She hadn't forgotten that the latest fire had started on a woman's farm.

"Really?" said Rusty. "Well, I suppose it takes all types. A chick is just as capable of chucking a match out a car window as anyone."

"I wonder how they have been lighting them?" said Jones. "I might have to ask…" but she trailed off. She had meant to say she would ask Atlas. Surely with all the interrogating he had been through overnight, the police would have revealed how the fires were started.

"How many ways are there to light a fire?" asked Chappy. "Matches. Cigarette lighter."

"Just like yours hey Phoenix!" Rusty laughed slapped Phoenix on the back.

Phoenix looked up, bewildered, and then held up his cigarette lighter, grinning. "Maybe I need to keep this out of sight for a while."

Jones looked around at the men who were all smiling and laughing. None of them seemed concerned with the fact that Phoenix was in fact holding a tool that could very well have lit these fires. Was there something she was missing? Was she jumping to conclusions, or were his friends too close to him to see what was right in front of them?

"Tossing a match out a window though," said Chappy. "That's unlikely to work. The flame'd blow out before it hit the ground. You'd have to light something else really, wouldn't ya?"

"What about a Molotov cocktail? Chuck one of them out the window into a crop or something, you'd have no hope!" suggested Rusty.

"That'd be pretty risky, wouldn't it?" said Hugo.

"I doubt a firebug is too worried about risk," Rusty replied.

"If that was used," said Jones. "I imagine it would be pretty easy for the police to find it and realise the fire was deliberately lit."

"I would have thought so," said Hugo. "Quinn said they were investigating all options. Maybe it wasn't something as obvious as a Molotov cocktail?"

"Or the police were just saying that," said Jones.

"And thinking about it," said Chappy. "If you were gonna choose to chuck a Molotov cocktail, or anything on fire for that matter, from a moving car, well I doubt you'd be driving. You'd have an accomplice I would reckon."

The group nodded and murmured in agreement. "So maybe it

wasn't thrown from a car. Maybe they parked somewhere?" suggested Hugo.

"Or walked somewhere?" said Jones. "Although if the fire took hold that would be pretty stupid."

"If it were me," said Phoenix. "I'd drive down some old track where no one could see me, and make sure I could flatten it out of there, in the opposite direction to the wind."

"You always were the smart one," said Chappy approvingly.

"That reminds me," said Jones, turning to Hugo. "You've never told me how you all met?"

"Ah, right," said Hugo. He looked around at the fellas but all of them were suddenly looking at their hands.

"Gosh, you've got me worried!" said Jones, before jokingly saying. "What? Were you all in prison together?"

Jones seemed to have hit some sort of nerve because they all started laughing and joking around in a way that made Jones feel uncomfortable. She felt her face turn red, wondering if she had said something wrong. She looked at Hugo and she watched him catch the eye of Chappy, Rusty and Phoenix in turn, who all gave him a slight nod. He had their permission.

Hugo turned to Jones, looked her in the eye, and then looked down. He was nervous. Jones felt her chest tighten. What on earth was he about to reveal?

"Well, we met each other at different times," said Hugo. "But in the end, we were all in the same unit."

"Unit?" asked Jones.

Hugo nodded. "We were all in the Special Forces. The SASR. Special Armed Services Regiment."

Jones looked at them all and then back at Hugo, a little unsure. "What, like commandos?"

"Kind of," said Hugo. "But we were more strategic. We did more reconnaissance and intelligence gathering."

"Wow," said Jones. "Gosh, I have no idea what that would have been liked, but it makes sense that you're all so close. But tough work?" She looked up into Hugo's eyes. She realised there was so much she didn't know about this man, but every time she learned something new, she became more fascinated by the type of person he was. This new information took that to another level.

Hugo nodded. "Very tough," he said. "And there's a lot we don't talk about. A lot we can't talk about. We went through quite a bit, and I'll tell you some of it at some point. But just know, there is nothing I wouldn't do for these three men here."

Jones felt her eyes pricking with tears. Rusty, Chappy and Phoenix were all looking at Hugo, nodding seriously. The bond between the four of them was palpable. It was similar to the bond she felt with Autumn, the physical feeling she had whenever she was near her sister.

She turned to Hugo and picked up his hands, clutching them. "Thank you. For telling me."

Hugo smiled, as their eyes locked.

"Alright! That's enough!" Chappy was clearly uncomfortable with the emotions in the room. "If you don't mind, I'm gonna jump in the shower."

The tension was gone. Hugo laughed, Rusty downed the last of his iced coffee, and Phoenix quietly stood and began straightening the couches where he and Chappy had slept.

As Jones and Hugo cleared the table, her mind was whirling. Atlas had been arrested, there was an arsonist in their community, and now she had discovered Hugo and his friends had been in the SASR. She didn't know how to process all of this information. All she could think of was that she needed to see her sister. She needed Autumn.

"I'm going to head off if that's alright?" Jones said to Hugo. "I want to get to the Bank, get organised. I think I might need to grab some more boxes of water and some food to have on hand. Plus I'm desperate to hear from Wren. Do you mind if I leave you all to it?"

Hugo pulled Jones into a hug. She needed it, and he obviously did too. He had sensed her mind was racing, and instinctively knew to pull her close. Jones leant into the hug and took a long, deep breath. Having his arms wrapped around her did seem to make her feel calmer. And stronger. As though whatever the day threw at her, she would be ok.

Jones leant back to look up at Hugo. She smiled, before pulling his head down. They kissed and then hugged again.

"I'll make sure the fellas tidy up before we leave," said Hugo.

"I'm not worried about that at all!" said Jones. She squeezed him tighter, before stepping back, smiling. "I'm just not a very good host, leaving."

"You're an amazing host!" said Hugo. "Plus, you let everyone sleep here with no issues. You've done more than enough."

"Ok, as long as you're sure," said Jones.

"You go," said Hugo. "The town needs you to be open. And I think Atlas needs you too."

"I really hope he's ok," said Jones, her smile vanishing.

"He will be," said Hugo. "With you on the case, you'll find out who did this."

Jones let out a short laugh and shook her head. "I appreciate your confidence in me! Although I'm not sure why everyone seems to think I'm going to solve this before the police do."

"You know exactly why everyone thinks that!" Hugo grinned and winked, before taking a damp cloth and moving over to wipe down the table.

Jones watched him for a moment. He really was remarkable, and with this new information, she knew she was going to discover a lot more amazing things about him. The SASR. Jones raised her eyebrows as she moved around the room, grabbing the things she would need for the day. She could only imagine the things he had gone through. How terrible had it been? Had he done anything she wouldn't understand?

Who was Hugo Gilbertson?

CHAPTER 27

Jones grunted as she dropped one of the water boxes on the top step of The Memory Bank. Pulling out the large, metal key, she opened the wooden door and quickly went to enter the alarm code.

"Autumn! Are you in here?"

"Of course I am!"

Jones's sister flew rapidly towards her, appearing from the wall of her escape room. Autumn's ghost form had discovered the secret room a few months ago. The door had been hidden behind a bookshelf, and Autumn herself, the previous custodian of The Memory Bank, and been none the wiser when it came to the room. She now called it her escape room because she could easily escape there, disappearing through its walls, and no one else could get in.

"You haven't spotted any flames?" Jones asked, pushing the box into the foyer.

"Nope, nothing," said Autumn. "But come on, I'm desperate. What's happening with Atlas?"

"Sorry, sorry," said Jones, walking to the counter and placing her purse and a bag of groceries on top. "Wren texted me to say his parents had taken him home."

"So he hasn't been charged?"

Jones shook her head. "Nope."

"Oh thank goodness," said Autumn.

"I don't think that means he's out of the woods."

"Yes, but it also means they don't have enough evidence. It buys us time."

"Us?"

"Don't start this again," said Autumn. "You know we're investigating. Just accept it. The Eldershaw Sisters Detective agency is on the case whether you like it or not."

"Well, the rest of the town seems to think so anyway."

"What do you mean?"

"Oh nothing," said Jones. "Just Hugo and Sybil are both taking it for granted them we, well I, am investigating."

"And so they should!" said Autumn. "We have got a pretty good track record, after all." She was smiling, hand on her hip and eyebrow raised.

"Well, before we become detectives, I've got to get everything out of my car and open up," said Jones.

She didn't mean to be dismissive, but Jones was beginning to feel frustrated by the fact that everyone was counting on her. Why on earth did everyone, including Autumn, think she could solve the mystery before the police? Wasn't it their job? Weren't they the experts? Why were all these people just assuming that she was investigating? And why were they all so sure Jones would discover the truth? She realised it wasn't all her. Autumn's ghostly skills had been crucial in her past successes, but no one else knew about Autumn. The weight of expectation was being firmly planted on her shoulders, and when the outcome had such importance to her friend, well, Jones wasn't sure she could handle the pressure.

Jones had quickly dropped into the Lilly Pilly Pantry on her way to work. She'd grabbed two boxes of water, a selection of snacks and some fruit, as well as some puzzle books. She thought there may be a lot of waiting time over the next few days, especially if the roads weren't opened.

"You're not old enough for crossword puzzles!" Autumn exclaimed when Jones pulled them out of the bag.

"Ha ha," said Jones. "Anyone can enjoy a crossword puzzle. Plus, if we have anyone hiding out in here again today, they may like them."

"Good idea," said Autumn. "Have any fire alerts come through?"

"Not yet, fortunately," said Jones, taking a glance at her phone. "Wouldn't it be nice to have a day with no alerts."

"I might head up to the roof and keep a lookout," said Autumn.

"Ok, but what if I need you?"

"Just call for me!" said Autumn.

"And what if there's someone here?"

Autumn nodded. "Good point. Well, how about I just keep popping in and out? I'll keep a watch up and down."

Jones smiled. The fact that she could take for granted her sister floating up through the ceiling and back bemused her. Oh, how her life had changed.

It was quiet, as she expected. She took the opportunity to organise some of the paperwork she had from recent deliveries, leaving a large pile for Atlas to enter into the system.

Atlas.

Jones picked up her phone but there were no updates. She didn't want to contact either Atlas or Wren in case they were both still sleeping. After such a long night, it was highly likely, although she did wonder how Atlas was feeling.

The time on her own meant her thoughts wandered to Hugo. The Special Forces? She would never have guessed that was the answer when she posed her question that morning. Although thinking now, he was a smart and fit man, so the reconnaissance and intelligence side made sense. But a solider? With a gun she presumed? She realised there was a lot she didn't know and may never know. However, what she had observed over the last few days was the loyalty of the four friends. How they all stuck together had to say something about each of them, and Hugo.

"What are you smiling about?" Autumn asked, floating down in front of Jones.

"Gosh, don't do that!" Jones brought her hand to her chest and let out a long sigh.

"Surely you're not scared of a ghost!"

"Well no, not a ghost," said Jones. "But any reasonable person would be scared to have someone sneak up on them and start talking loudly.

"So, what was it? Hugo, I'm guessing." Autumn perched herself on the tall boy next to where Jones was rearranging a display of tabs that many customers had requested to use in annotating their books and bullet journals.

Jones couldn't help but roll her eyes. Mainly because Autumn was right and she knew the look on her face would make that clear to her sister.

"Ooooh," she sang. "Anything new, or just the usual mushy stuff?"

"Well, I do have some new information," said Jones. "Although I'm not quite sure I'm ready to share it." Jones was only teasing. Of course, she would tell Autumn, but the look on her face was priceless.

"What!" Autumn flew directly up and then zoomed down to face Jones. "What is it? You have to tell me!"

"It's kind of private," said Jones, hiding a slight smile by moving to another table to adjust a set of bronze horse head bookends.

"Come on! Who am I going to tell?" Autumn was exasperated. Jones shook her head, grinning.

"Is it bad? Or is it about the fires?" Autumn was darting around, trying to catch a glimpse of Jones's face as she reacted to her guesses. "Oh, I know! It's about Phoenix. You spoke with Hugo about him being the arsonist!"

"Well, no, not exactly," said Jones. "But we were all talking about the arsonist and the blokes were trying to guess how it was done. Everyone pointed at Phoenix's lighter and started laughing."

"What? You think they're all in on it?"

Jones laughed and shook her head, adjusting a pile of family history books. "No, not at all. They were joking because there was no way any of them even dreamed Phoenix did it. Just that they might start looking at him if he kept waving his lighter around."

"But what about you? Do you think he could have done it?"

"I still don't have any idea," said Jones. "But...."

"What? Oh, come on Jones! You're driving me crazy!"

Jones finally stopped and looked at her sister. "Well, I found out how they all know each other."

"And?" Autumn's eyebrows were high.

"They were all in the Special Forces. The Special Armed Forces Regiment."

"What, so they were soldiers?"

Jones nodded. "Yes, but they were in an elite group. Hugo said they worked on intelligence and reconnaissance."

"Oh, so like spy missions?"

"I don't think quite like that," said Jones. "But he didn't say much. We were with all the guys, and I think it was a big deal just to share that much."

"Why?" Autumn tilted her head.

"I don't know," said Jones. "They're all very close, and I imagine they've been through some things that are hard to talk about. It felt special, you know. It was like they all permitted Hugo to tell me. I was being let into the group or something. It's silly, I know." Jones walked over to the counter, feeling awkward in front of Autumn.

"It's not silly at all!" says Autumn. "It sounds lovely."

Jones nodded. It was. And then her phone beeped.

Picking it up, she saw it was Wren.

Atlas has asked if you'll come and visit him at his parents. They want to talk to you.

"Atlas and his parents want to talk to me," said Jones, turning to Autumn with a frown.

"That's good, isn't it?"

Jones let out a long breath. "I guess so. It just sounds, I don't know, ominous somehow."

"I'm sure it will be fine," said Autumn.

Jones couldn't put her finger on why the message made her feel uncomfortable. She just hoped everything was ok.

CHAPTER 28

Jones pushed the door open to Hugo's. There were a few people sitting at the tables, eating meals and chatting quietly. She walked up to the bar and waited for Hugo.

She hadn't wanted to close up The Memory Bank. But there was no one else to stay. She wasn't worried about the customers, but she was concerned that if things took a turn for the worse, the oldies would arrive on her doorstep again only to discover no one was there.

"Hello there," said Hugo, smiling as he walked out of the kitchen.

"Hi," Jones smiled. "Quiet I see."

Hugo glanced around. "Yep, but it's only just eleven. Hopefully, the word will have gotten around about my special lunch menu."

"You rang Sybil then?"

He laughed. "Of course! Quickest way. Can I get you anything?"

"Oh no, thanks. I was hoping you don't mind doing me a favour though?"

"Anything!"

"Well, I've taken the liberty of putting a sign on The Memory Bank directing anyone who needs a safe place to stay, to come in here. Is that ok? It's just Atlas has asked me to come visit."

"Absolutely," said Hugo, leaning on the bar. "But is Atlas ok?"

"I think so," said Jones. "But I don't know anything more. Wren just messaged saying Atlas and his parents wanted to talk to me."

Hugo nodded. "Ok. Well, I hope it's good news."

"To be honest, I'm not quite sure what I'm walking into. I've never really met Atlas's parents. I've got no idea what they think of me."

"Surely they would have only heard good things. You were the person they called when Atlas needed someone. You rushed to the police station last night when they couldn't. I bet they just want to thank you."

Jones smiled, not having thought of that. "You could be right. I hope you're right."

"Hey, I've got a lemon tart out the back. It's from yesterday, but would you like to maybe take that along?"

Jones knew there was a reason she liked this man. "That's a lovely idea. Thank you."

Hugo wouldn't let her pay, saying it wasn't fresh, and he wanted Atlas and his family to have it. She waved goodbye from the door, as he served the couple who had come up to pay for their meals.

Jones stood outside and took a deep breath. She was happy to notice that the air seemed fresher, the smoke hopefully shifting. It was still hot, but the atmosphere didn't feel quite as threatening as it had yesterday. She saw cars travelling down Main Street and guessed the police were now letting people back in. These both felt like positive signs.

Driving in the direction of Atlas and his parents, Jones was still feeling apprehensive. She was very thankful for Hugo's lemon tart to break the ice, but she had no idea what she would be walking into. How would Atlas be, having spent the night under interrogation by the police? She imagined his parents would be feeling lost and hopeless, although she knew Wren would be supporting them. But why did they want to see Jones in particular? What could she do to help?

Then she realised. They would be more people asking her to solve the mystery. Asking her to come up with the answers. Jones gulped, feeling a sense of dread, of letting everyone down, especially Atlas. Tears sprang into her eyes. It was too much. She had too much on her plate, as well as being part of a town that was almost consumed by fire just the day before. She had no idea how to solve this although she desperately wanted to. Realistically, there was nothing she could do. So how could she break that to Atlas and his parents?

"Don't be ridiculous, Jones!" she said out loud. "You're making yourself out to be more important than you are," she continued in her head. "They probably just want to talk about Atlas, what's happening with his work and what the police said. They're not expecting you to walk in and work miracles."

Jones shook her head and rolled back her shoulders. "Pull yourself together." She found she was putting herself into the frame of mind when going to a particularly hard interview. Jones had covered a lot of tragedy and devastating stories as a journalist. She hoped what Atlas and his parents had to say was nothing close to this, but she found it helpful to go into journalist mode, running the questions she would ask through her head, anticipating the answers, and how she would handle each possible variation. It may have been useless for this particular situation, but it stopped her being so self-involved and focused on the task at hand.

A black tractor tyre with the name Hemmings marked the entrance to the family's farm. The track was rutted and bumpy, and Jones took it very slowly in her Mini. She drove through scraggly bushes and trees before she was met with rows of agapanthus on either side. Turning a slight bend, she was pleased to see a neat and tidy brown brick farmhouse. The garden was full of native plants, bordered by a low mesh fence. As she stepped out of the car, holding the lemon tart, she heard a dog yapping. A brown and white terrier came bursting from the side of the house to greet her.

"Spike! Spike!" a man's voice called. "Spike, get over here!" The little dog stopped barking but didn't move away from Jones. He darted back and forth in front of her as Jones made her way to the man who was waiting, desperately trying not to trip over the dog or drop the tart.

"Sorry about him. Not as well trained as the sheepdogs, that's for sure!" He reached his hand out. "Dave. You must be Jones."

Jones shook his hand. "Nice to meet you."

He turned, leading her to the front door and into a cool and dark hallway. "Come through. Everyone's out the back."

Dave opened a doorway at the end of the hall which presented her with a lovely big and bright room. The floor was terracotta tiles, with a blue kitchen in the corner to the left, and a large, round dining table to the right. Jones saw an old woman in a rocking chair, knitting needles clacking. On one couch was a teenage girl who Jones guessed to be Atlas's sister, Maia. And on the couch opposite, Jones presumed was Atlas's mother. She sat next to a figure that was lying down, curled up tightly in a crocheted blanket, despite the hot weather.

Atlas.

CHAPTER 29

"Tammy," said Dave. "Jones is here."

The woman turned and quickly got up from the couch. The slim woman with short brown hair made a beeline for Jones and wrapped her into a huge hug. If she hadn't been so shocked, Jones would have let out a sigh of relief. Instead, she frantically tried to balance the tart in one hand.

"Careful Tam! She's holding something!"

Tammy pulled back. "Oh sorry! Sorry!"

Jones thrust the pie towards Atlas's mum. "It's a lemon tart. From Hugo's. He thought you might like it."

"Oh lovely," said Tammy. "Perfect. We love lemon, don't we mum!" Tammy called out, looking at the woman in the rocking chair.

"Very thoughtful," the woman said, smiling at Jones but not getting up from her rocking chair. She was wearing a t-shirt, tracksuit pants, and a pair of sandals. Jones saw there was a walking stick leaning against the chair. She glanced at the hidden figure of Atlas on the couch, but he still hadn't moved.

"Can I get you a coffee, Jones? Or a tea?" asked Tammy, putting her hand on Jones's back, and guiding her over to the kitchen. Dave took Tammy's place on the couch.

"A tea was it?" Tammy asked, taking the kettle to the sink to refill it.

"Yes, a tea would be lovely."

"How do you have it?"

"White with one please."

Tammy set the kettle on to boil and then pulled mugs out of the cupboard. She grabbed everything she needed, and, as she placed tea bags in the mugs, she began to speak quietly.

"He's not doing too well, Jones."

"I can see. Poor guy. Was it awful, at the police station?"

"Awful's a word for it," said Tammy, looking up at Jones. "They've treated him like dirt, from what I've gathered. Why they've got it out for my son I have no idea. You know him. There's no way he would do anything like this."

"Of course not," said Jones, her voice raising a little louder than she had meant it to. She glanced over towards the others, who quickly looked away, not wanting to appear to be listening to every word they were saying. "It's almost as though this Candace woman has it out for him. Or someone does."

"That's exactly what I said to Dave," Tammy said, still doing her best to keep her voice low. "And who else would point the finger but the actual arsonist! Why aren't the police interrogating her?"

The kettle had finished boiling. Tammy snatched it up and accidentally sloshed a large amount of boiling water in and around the mug she had it aimed at. "Oh golly, look at me. I can't seem to pull myself together."

"Here, let me," said Jones. She grabbed a tea towel that was hanging on the stove and started mopping up, before taking the kettle from Tammy. "I'll fix these. Milk and sugar for all of them?"

"Yes, thank you. Yes, Dave has two sugars, and mum only a half."

Jones finished the tea while Tammy kept filling Jones in on the events of the past twenty-four hours.

"They had him in the Lilly Pilly Creek Station for hours before they called us," she said.

"Really?" Jones was surprised to hear this, thinking Christopher would have at least called his parents.

"It's those city detectives. They've got a bee in their bonnet. Want to make quick work of this whole business. But that just means they're not listening to locals, and not doing their job properly. Meanwhile, the real firebug is out there, probably still at it!"

Jones shook her head, as she handed two of the cups to Tammy. "I didn't make one for Maia. Or Atlas."

Tammy shook her head. "No, Maia doesn't drink tea. And Atlas hasn't had anything since he got home. Barely spoken, except to ask for you."

Jones was a little taken aback by this. "Oh, ok."

Jones brought the tea over to Tammy's mum.

"Thank you, dear. I'm Rhoda."

"Sorry Mum," said Tammy. "Jones, my mum lives with us. We've all been up most of the night. You had a bit of a nap, didn't you, Mum?"

"Dozed off in my chair at some stage," she said. "Thanks for the tea. Tammy, why don't you cut up the tart? I think we could all use a piece."

"Yes, good idea!"

"I'll do it, Tam," said Dave, standing so his wife could take his place. "Sit down and talk to Jones. Atlas, why don't you sit up? Jones is here."

"Leave him, Dave," said Tammy, but then the crocheted bundle next to her started to move.

Jones sat next to his sister, smiling and quietly said hello. Maia smiled but didn't say anything.

After Jones took a sip of her tea and placed it on the coffee table in front of them, she looked up at Atlas who had risen to a seated position. She was shocked. His hair was a mess, he wasn't wearing his glasses, and had what could only be described as a four o'clock shadow. His eyes were drawn, and he was very, very pale.

"Hi Atlas," Jones said. "This is all a bit crap, isn't it."

Atlas tried to smile, but his mouth formed more of a grimace. "Bloody crap." He ran his hand through his hair, causing it to stand on end even more. Jones glanced at Maia and they shared a small smile but neither said a word.

"So, what did the police say? Are you in the clear?"

Atlas snorted. "Not likely. Not unless they find the real arsonist. For now, I'm it!"

"Oh Atlas," said Jones. "What can I do? Shall I speak to Christopher? Surely there's more he can do."

"I doubt it," he said. "Christopher pushed as hard as he could, but the detectives wouldn't listen. Thought they knew better. Thought I'd pulled the wool over his eyes. Idiots." He rolled his eyes.

"But they don't have any evidence," said David. "Why are they so sure it's you?"

Tammy came over and placed saucers of the lemon tart on the coffee table, and also handed one to Rhoda.

"Beats me!" said Atlas. "The only thing they kept saying was they have matching tyre tracks. That my car has been seen in the area. But it hasn't been! It was either at home, at the station, or The Memory Bank. I haven't been anywhere else!"

"Wish Lilly Pilly Creek had CCTV footage," said Tammy, sitting back with her plate. Everyone looked at her, surprised. "What? That's what they do, isn't it? It's what they do on TV anyway." She took a bite of her tart and shrugged.

"Course they do," said Rhoda, clacking her needles. "Just not in a small town like ours. Useless. Not that I want them watching my every move. But it'd sure help us now."

"There might be another way," said Jones. "What type of car do you have again?"

"A little Toyota," said Atlas. "Blue."

"As common as muck!" said Dave.

"Yes, that's true. There are a lot of those little cars around. Surely they're looking into that. Checking all similar cars registered in the area?"

Atlas shrugged and slumped back onto the couch.

"Is there anything else you can think of Jones?" asked Tammy. "What would you normally do?"

"Normally do?" Jones asked.

"You know," said Tammy. "When you've investigated before. What would you do next?"

"Oh, well, ah, I'm just a journalist. I'm not like an investigator or anything."

"No need to be modest around us, Jones," said Rhoda. "Atlas here has told us everything. We know you're the one who got to the bottom of that mess with Lorne. Not to mention poor Iris Cartwright."

"And your sister of course," said Tammy, shaking her head. "Dreadful. But you caught that nasty boyfriend of hers. What was his name again?"

"Jamie. Jamie Royce," Jones said, picking up her piece of tart and taking a bite. "But all of it was just happenstance. I didn't know what I was doing. Things just seemed to fall into my lap." Jones was probably playing things down a bit. But no one knew about Autumn and what she could do. And the last thing she wanted to do was to get the hopes up of the Hemming family.

She glanced at Atlas, who smiled at her. "It's ok Jones. I know you'd help if you could. But at the moment, I seem like a bit of a lost cause."

Dave patted his son firmly on the leg. "Well, we're not giving up that easily. If we all put our heads together, I'm sure we'll work something out. At this stage, it seems like the car's the best lead we've got."

"Atlas, do you think there's anyone else in the CFS who could have done it?" asked Jones. "It's just that everyone seems so sure it must be someone connected to the fire service. Anyone else that comes off a bit strange to you?"

Atlas shook his head. "It's so hard to say. I don't know anyone that well. The person I've spent the most time with is Candace because she's been training me. And of course, she's the one who's accused me of this."

"Horrible woman," said Rhoda.

"Mum, come on, you've never met her," said Tammy. "She's not done right by Atlas, but I don't know. Maybe she's just doing her job."

"Ha! Or maybe she's trying to frame my grandson!"

Jones turned to Atlas. "Do you think it's possible? Could it be Candace?"

Atlas frowned. "I honestly don't know. She's just as likely as anyone else, as far as I know."

"What sorta car does she have?" Dave asked.

"Um," Atlas looked up at the ceiling. "I think some sort of four-wheel drive. White maybe. Nothing like my car."

"Well, that doesn't mean she doesn't have access to a car like yours," said Tammy. "Maybe someone in her family has one like it. Jones, could you look into that?"

Jones wanted to reign Tammy in. Stop her presuming Jones was going to solve this. But she couldn't. She wanted to sort this out as much as everyone else in this room. It was a good lead. She felt like she was in a television mystery series, and had to admit she was getting swept up in this new storyline.

"I can look into it," said Jones. "I can't promise anything, but I can see what I can find out."

"Excellent!" said Rhoda, before taking a large mouthful of the tart.

"Is there anything else I can do?" asked Jones. "Is Wren helping you with all the legal stuff?"

Dave nodded. "She's organising one of her lawyer mates to speak with us. They're criminal lawyers. Wren said it's all a bit above her pay grade, but she says he's a good bloke."

"That's good," said Jones. "I'm sure Wren has it handled. And what about work Atlas? Can I help with that?"

"Well, the CFS has suspended me, so I'm not gonna be out fighting fires anytime soon. No excuses now not to be in the office."

"Oh Atlas," said Tammy. "You don't need to rush back to work. This has all been a bit of a shock. Your clients will understand.'

"I know Mum," said Atlas. "I know. But what else am I gonna do?"

"Just make sure you look after yourself," said Jones. "Maybe wait until you hear what this new lawyer has to say. Then worry about work. If anyone comes into the Bank I'll just let them know you're unwell. Ok?"

"Ok, thanks Jones," Atlas said. "I suppose we should make sure we have time for this lawyer guy."

"Good," said Jones. "And if I hear anything, anything at all, I'll let you know right away."

The room went quiet. There wasn't much more to say. Everyone sipped their tea, ate their lemon tart, and did their best to appear hopeful.

Jones said her goodbyes and insisted she would find her way out.

"Maia, can you just go with Jones and make sure Spike stays in the yard," said Tammy.

As Jones and the teenager walked outside, Maia put her hand on

Jones's arm.

"Atlas will be ok, won't he?"

Jones looked at Maia, hesitating before replying. "If I have anything to say about it."

Maia smiled and bent down to pick up Spike who had been hovering at their feet.

Jones reversed her Mini away from the house and waved goodbye to Maia.

She only hoped there was something she could do.

CHAPTER 30

The bar was quiet when she walked in. Hugo was behind the bar, drying glasses whilst a small group of firefighters finished their schnitzels.

"A bit quieter than you expected?" Jones asked as she slid onto a bar stool.

"There were a few more earlier," said Hugo. "But they're all exhausted. I think most have headed home to bed."

Jones smiled and then turned her head sharply as something caught her eye in her peripheral vision. Autumn had flown in and was now sitting next to her at the bar.

"I saw you from the roof," said Autumn, winking.

"How was Atlas?" Hugo asked.

"Not in a good way at all," said Jones, relieved to see Hugo hadn't noticed she'd been communicating with a ghost. "Curled up in the fetal position, literally, when I arrived."

"Poor bloke," said Hugo. "It's not fair."

"No it's not," said Jones. "And he seems certain I'm going to be able to fix it. His whole family thinks I'll be able to find out who did this."

"You do have a knack for these things," said Hugo, nodding his head.

"But that's all just by accident," said Jones. "And no one was depending on me. Everything just fell into place. But with this one, all we know is the police say Atlas's car was sighted, that his tyre tracks were there, except he is adamant he was nowhere near the fires."

"Of course he wasn't," said Hugo. "Did he know how it started? Did the police tell him?"

"Bugger, I forgot to ask him." Jones put her head in her hands. After leaving the Hemmings, Jones had started to believe that perhaps there was something she could do to help. But the more she thought about it, the more lost she felt.

"Well, it's likely he doesn't know," said Hugo. "I haven't heard anyone in today say they know how the fires were started, so perhaps the police are keeping things very close to their chest."

"Which means there is only one person I can ask," said Jones. "I promised Atlas I'd go and speak to Christopher. I think I'm going to have to."

Hugo nodded and called out "Thanks a lot!" to the group of firefighters as they left. It was now just Hugo, Jones, Autumn and one other couple in the bar.

"Do you have any suspects?" he asked.

"Do you think I should?" Jones asked, shrugging her shoulders.

Hugo smiled. "If I know you, you've at least thought about it. Come on, give me a hint!"

Jones couldn't help but laugh a little. "Grab me a lemon lime and bitters first, please."

"Sure thing!"

Hugo turned to grab a tall glass from the shelf. Jones watched as he shovelled the ice in and splashed the bitters on top. He added some lime cordial, topped it with lemonade, and then hung a slice of lime on the rim before sliding it to Jones with a straw.

"Voila!"

"Thank you!" said Jones, taking a long sip. "Ahhh, good stuff."

"What was that?"

"Oh, that's what dad taught us!" Autumn said loudly, laughing.

Jones smiled and looked up at Hugo. "It's what my Dad taught Autumn and me. We always used to say it when we had a fizzy drink. For some reason, I just remembered it."

Hugo nodded in appreciation. "Alright, enough distractions. What's your suspect list?"

She sighed, took a long sip, and began. "Well, there's a few. Possibly one of the farmers where the fires started."

"Sure, sure. Maybe one was on the arsonist's property and one was a distraction, perhaps?" said Hugo.

Jones nodded. "Yep. Insurance or some sort of cover-up?"

"You do know that's Sally Butler over there, with her husband," said Hugo.

Jones spun around on her stool. A young woman wearing jeans, brown boots and a t-shirt was sitting eating at the table opposite a broad man wearing the fluorescent orange shirt of a tradie of some sort.

"What do you know about her?" Jones asked Hugo, attempting a slight nod at Autumn who immediately flew over to them. She turned back to face Hugo, darting glances in the couple's direction.

"Not much actually," said Hugo. "I can't remember her ever coming in before. She must have heard about the special lunch deal and decided to support us. I guess it was the CFS who protected her farm."

Jones nodded, thinking. Would an arsonist intentionally visit a bar that would be full of the same firefighters who controlled the blaze? She had to admit that so far she had no luck getting in the mind of an arsonist, so anything was possible.

"She doesn't look like much of an arsonist to me," said Hugo.

"No, she doesn't," said Jones. "But then again I have no idea what an arsonist looks like."

Hugo watched the couple for a few seconds before turning back to Jones. "Who else?"

Jones glanced around the bar, just to double check no one else was there before she shared the next name. "Well, I've already mentioned Candace Chadwick. She does seem to have it in for Atlas."

"Yep, I suppose she could be trying to frame him. And she would know all the right things to say to the police. She sounds like a pretty firm contender."

"Yes, that's what I thought. But I have no idea where to start with her."

"Anyone else?"

Jones hesitated.

"Go on," said Autumn. "Run your Phoenix theory by him. I'm sure he'll understand."

"What is it?" asked Hugo, placing the glass he had been wiping down on the counter. "Jones?"

Jones couldn't take her eyes off her hands wrapped around her glass. It didn't feel right, to accuse one of Hugo's friends. But if she was going to help Atlas, and help him avoid jail, then she had to do everything in her power to discover the truth. He was depending on her.

"I'm not sure how to say this," said Jones. "And please, I want you to understand where I'm coming from. I'm just trying to help Atlas. I don't want to hurt anyone."

Hugo frowned, nodding slightly. "Ok. Who?"

"Be confident," said Autumn. "He's been carrying around that lighter. He's an obvious choice. You have every right to ask."

"Phoenix," said Jones, raising her eyes to Hugo's.

His mouth was wide. "You can't be serious!"

Jones shrugged. "The cigarette lighter. He's rather mysterious. And now that I know about his past, well, it's not that much of a stretch, is it?"

Hugo turned away from Jones and started noisily replacing glasses on the shelf.

"Hugo? What do you think?"

"I think you are way off base. There is no chance Phoenix has anything to do with it. Do not mention it again."

Jones was shocked. She knew Hugo would be protective of his friend, but she thought he would surely see why he was on her list.

"Ok, ok," said Jones. "But you have to admit, it wouldn't be surprising that I might consider him?"

"That's enough Jones," said Hugo, turning to face her, his face filled with anger. "I don't want to talk about this anymore. I think it's best if you leave."

Jones's stomach dropped. She felt her lip start to quiver, but before she let her emotions get the better of her, she rolled back her shoulders and pushed her glass away from her.

"Ok, if that's what you want," said Jones. "Goodbye."

Hopping off the stool, she grabbed her handbag and walked directly out the door of the bar, resisting the urge to glance back.

"Jeepers, you sure hit a nerve!" said Autumn as she flew after Jones. "That makes me even more suspicious of Phoenix."

"Leave it, Autumn," said Jones. "Please just leave it."

"Alright," said Autumn. "But Phoenix has every right to be on our suspect list. Until we're proven otherwise."

Pulling out her key, Jones opened the Bank, turned off the alarm, and made her way towards the garden doors. "That's enough Autumn. I think I need to be alone."

"I understand," said Autumn, watching Jones walk away. "I'll call if anyone comes in."

Jones opened the glass door out to their garden and closed it behind her. Making her way to the area called the Secret Garden, she sat on a cast iron garden seat in the shade, put her head in her hands, and let the tears that had been brimming all day, flow down her cheeks.

The stress of the fires, Atlas's arrest, and now feeling Hugo's anger for the first time, was too much. Not to mention the months of drama since Autumn's death. She would be forgiven for going home to bed and staying there. It was very tempting.

But Atlas needed her. He was depending on her and Autumn, although he didn't know it, to discover the truth. She had to focus. There would be time to fall in a heap later.

CHAPTER 31

"Do you mind if I come out?" asked Autumn. She was poking her head through the lattice next to Jones where a clematis was growing. It was somewhat disturbing to see, but did make Jones smile.

"You do know how to freak a person out," said Jones.

"I do my best," said Autumn, slowly bringing her entire body through to Jones's side. She sat in a chair opposite her sister. "How are you feeling?"

"Utterly overwhelmed, to be honest."

"The last few days have been a lot," said Autumn. "I know it's partly my fault, but it isn't really up to you to save Atlas. That's the police's job."

"I know, I know," said Jones. "But everyone seems to think I'll work it out before them."

"And you know what, you probably would," said Autumn. "But that doesn't mean they won't work it out eventually. You've got to look after yourself."

"Hugo hates me," said Jones. "And rightfully so. What was I thinking?"

"You mean, what were we thinking? I thought it would be a good idea too. I thought he'd understand."

"We completely underestimated the friendship in that group," said Jones. "I mean they're special forces for goodness sake. Just imagine what they've gone through together. Of course, Hugo wasn't going to throw Phoenix under the bus, no matter how clear the signs are."

"Well, you couldn't have known that," said Autumn. "He's looking out for his friend. But you're looking out for your friend too. I bet if Hugo was in your shoes he would have done the same thing."

"And I probably would have hated him for it too," said Jones, letting out a sob.

"I'm sure he'll understand, eventually," said Autumn.

"He still might not want to have anything to do with me," said Jones.

"Don't worry. I don't think we're there yet. He adores you. This is your first fight. Let him calm down."

"For how long? And what do I do in the meantime?"

"Well, you know what I'm going to suggest. But it's up to you. Do what's best for you."

"You think we should keep investigating, don't you?"

Autumn shrugged. "Only if you're ok with that," she replied. "I do honestly think we make a pretty unstoppable team, but it has to feel right. I think you need to take some time to decide what feels right to you."

Jones leant back in the chair and looked up into the sky. The smoky haze that had been there was all but cleared, the startling blue sky making a comeback. She could feel sweat behind her knees, and despite the shade, she was feeling hot, and quite bothered.

"I think it's time for me to go home," said Jones. "I think I need a cool shower and an afternoon nap. I know everything always seems so much worse when I'm tired."

"I think that's a great idea," said Autumn. "It doesn't seem like any fire emergencies are imminent. We can regroup in the morning."

Jones stood up, stretched her arms above her head, and made her way back into the Bank. "Here's hoping there's no one in my house when I get home. I could do with some peace."

After walking inside, Jones did little more than turn off the lights and grab her bag.

"Look after yourself, Jones," said Autumn. "I'll see you in the morning."

"Thanks," said Jones.

"Oh, and Jones," said Autumn.

"Yes?"

"Just so you know, I didn't hear much of interest between Sally Butler and her husband," she said.

Jones had completely forgotten about them.

"They did spend a lot of time chatting about the damage to their farm," Autumn continued. "And what they needed to do to keep functioning. They did mention insurance, but I guess they would anyway."

"Yes, I suppose so," said Jones.

"Look, you get out of here. Not important. Just thought I should mention it."

"Thanks, Autumn."

Jones waved, locked up and got into her car. She paused for a moment, glancing across to Hugo's. A few people were inside drinking. She was happy for him. She hoped he had a busy night. It was tempting to text him, but she thought better of it. He had asked her to leave. He needed space. If she hadn't heard from him tomorrow, she would reach out. But for now, she just wanted to get home, take a cool shower, and curl up in bed. After a night of little sleep. She was exhausted.

The guilt of telling Hugo that Phoenix was on her suspect list wouldn't abate. She regretted saying something. But then, would a lie have been better? The thing was, on paper Phoenix was a credible suspect. He came across as moody and aloof, he played with a cigarette lighter constantly, and now Jones knew that he had been in the army, which had no doubt impacted his mental health in some way. If it wasn't for Hugo, she would have gone directly to Christopher and presented her theory.

Then she remembered Atlas. Perhaps, just like Phoenix, he looked equally credible to the detectives. A smart guy, still living at home with his parents, new to the CFS, and apparently with a car that had been spotted near the crime scenes. Jones of course knew better than the Police. Perhaps Hugo knew better than she did? Maybe she needed to take Hugo's opinion into account. Hugo believed Phoenix was as incapable of this as Atlas. And yet Jones couldn't dismiss Phoenix entirely. Not until she had more information.

At home, Jones poured a chilled glass of Pino Grigio and sipped it as she got in the shower. Yes, it was wine in the shower time, and she soaked it in. The cool water ran down her back, taking away the heat and dampening the emotions that had been running through her. By the time she was finished, the combination had relaxed her and she lay on her bed. It was only around three in the afternoon, but she knew sleep was what she needed.

Yet, as she lay there, the fan above her doing its best to lull her, she couldn't stop thinking about Hugo and Atlas and the mess she seemed to be in. No matter how much she tried to push it out of her mind, she knew it was inevitable. She was going to investigate the fires, for Atlas's sake. Even if that meant investigating one of her boyfriend's best friends in the process.

If Hugo was the man she thought he was, he would understand.

CHAPTER 32

"Jones! Wake up!"

Jones shook her head. Her eyes were heavy and it took a long time for her to focus on where the voice was coming from.

"Autumn? What is it? What's wrong?"

"There's another fire," said Autumn.

Sitting immediately up, Jones found her mouth was agape. "What time is it? What day is it?"

"You've slept through the night," said Autumn. "It's Thursday, just after seven in the morning."

"And another fire has started already?"

"Yes!" said Autumn. "Although I don't know if it's been reported yet. I spotted it from my lookout."

"Is it close?" Jones had gotten out of bed and was now looking at her phone. Autumn was right. There were no alerts yet.

"No, I think it's near Lobethal again, or in that vicinity. Maybe it's just a flare-up?"

"Surely the CFS are still out that way," said Jones. "They'd be monitoring for spot fires, wouldn't they?"

Jones made her way into the bathroom, slightly taken aback by the state of her hair after going to sleep with it wet. She started trying to push it into shape, before brushing her teeth.

"What are you doing?" asked Autumn.

"I've got to get to the Bank. People might need me."

"Ok, well I don't think we need to panic just yet," said Autumn.

"Then why have you woken me up so early?"

"Fair point," said Autumn. "I am a bit on edge. It's already quite warm and windy out there. It is a terrible fire day."

Jones nodded the toothbrush in her mouth. Today was the catastrophic day they had forecasted.

"Well, I'd rather be prepared," said Jones. "I've slept enough. I can't believe I fell asleep at three yesterday afternoon!"

"You needed it," said Autumn. "Feeling better?"

"I'm not sure yet," said Jones. "I've just been woken from a deep sleep and am yet to visit Sybil. Talk to me after my first coffee."

"Right, well, you get dressed, and I'll meet you in the car."

Jones found a pair of denim shorts and a blue t-shirt stating *The only thing predictable about life is its unpredictability.*' as declared by Remy the Rat in Ratatouille. She put on a pair of sneakers, and despairing at her hair, threw it into a ponytail and popped on a cap. Rubbing SPF moisturiser into her face, she took a deep breath, ready to face the day.

"Do you know where Sybil's parked today?" Jones asked, sliding into the driver's seat.

"Actually," said Autumn. "She's right outside The Memory Bank."

Jones laughed as she reversed. "Perfect! I'm taking that as a positive sign."

"A positive sign for what?"

"For everything! The day, the fire, Atlas."

"Hugo?" Autumn said, glancing at Jones.

"Sure, Hugo too!"

It wasn't long before they were parked in front of The Memory

Bank, immediately behind Sybil's coffee van.

"Oh Sybil, why don't you park here every day!" cried Jones.

"Well, I guess that means you're ok with it?" Sybil said, pouring milk into her silver jug.

"Ok! I'm delighted! Gosh, imagine how many coffees I can have today now I only have to walk out the front door!"

Autumn laughed alongside Jones and Sybil.

"But I thought you were leaving town today?" asked Jones.

"I am," said Sybil. "Just thought I'd cover the morning rush and then head out. Any update on Atlas?"

Jones felt her positive mood start to abate. "He's home, which is a relief. But he's not in a good state. His whole family's worried. It sounds like the police don't have any other suspects."

"Do you?" Sybil raised her eyebrows and Jones rolled her eyes.

"I'm not sure why everyone, including Atlas's whole family, seems to think I'm investigating this and have any ability whatsoever to solve it!"

"Of course, that's the police's job," said Sybil. "It's just that you do seem to have a knack for solving the mysteries of Lilly Pilly Creek."

"Hah!" said Autumn. "I wonder why that is!"

With a smile, Jones responded to Sybil. "I'm not sure if it's a knack or just good luck. And I'm not feeling particularly lucky at the moment."

"All I'll say is, I'm sure Atlas would appreciate anything you can do, and I'll help you as much as I can."

"Thanks, Sybil," said Jones. "To be honest you've been crucial in the past. You seem to know everything about Lilly Pilly Creek."

As Sybil swirled the milk into Jones's flat white she said, "That's just luck too. Funny how open people are with their conversations whilst they wait for coffee, as though no one else is listening."

"Hugo finds that too," said Jones, feeling somewhat uncomfortable speaking of him so normally after yesterday's fight.

"The magic of a bartender!" said Sybil, handing Jones not only her coffee but a ham and cheese croissant, reading Jones's mind.

"I'll be back!" said Jones, swiping her card before walking to The Memory Bank door. "Thank you!"

"Are you going to speak to Hugo, do you think?" asked Autumn as they entered the Bank.

It was cool in the Bank and Jones decided to pull the blinds down over the glass doors to the garden, to keep it that way.

"Yes, of course," said Jones. "I'm just hoping he comes to me first. But I will. I can't just leave it."

"Hopefully he comes and apologises," says Autumn.

"Or maybe I should be the one apologising?" said Jones. "I mean, we're furious that the police think Atlas could have done this. Why shouldn't Hugo feel the same way?"

"He can feel however he likes," said Autumn. "That doesn't make Phoenix less likely to be a suspect."

"Maybe it does," shrugged Jones. "I'm not sure what to think."

"What we need to do is put our detective hats on and come up with a strategy," said Autumn, who of course in that moment made her deerstalker appear on her head.

Jones sighed. "I suppose you're right. I'm just not feeling in the zone."

"Did you ever not write a story because you weren't in the zone? Or did you just do it anyway?"

"All I'll say is, the story always got written, it just depends if I left it until right on my deadline or not!"

"Well, we don't know what Atlas's deadline will be, so we need to get cracking."

"Gosh, you're a hard taskmaster!" Jones took a long sip of her coffee. She was hoping it would have some magic effect on her current outlook, but aside from being delicious, she felt no change.

"Grab your notebook and fountain pen." Autumn had zoomed over to the counter.

Jones followed, walking behind and pulling the notebook from her hiding place at the back of the shelf. She realised she should probably be using the lockbox she had at her disposal.

"Let's start with the suspects," said Autumn, and Jones folded back the cover of the notebook, flattening it.

"Right, so, we have Phoenix, Candace, the two farmers," said Jones. "What were their names?"

"Rhys and um, I think it was Sally, ah, Sally Butler."

"Ok, Rhys Bauer and Sally Butler," said Jones. "And I suppose we need to put Atlas."

"He's not our suspect!" said Autumn, folding her arms across her chest and frowning.

"Of course not," said Jones. "I'll put an asterix next to his name if that makes you feel better. But I think we need to consider why the police have Atlas as the main suspect and work out how to disprove it."

Autumn sighed and nodded. "Yes, of course, you're right."

"So, with that being said, let's address the motive and the evidence," said Jones.

"Lack of evidence you mean," said Autumn. "Is it right that the only thing they have to place Atlas at the scene is a possible sighting of a car similar to his?"

"Yep," said Jones. "And the tyre tracks. We need to find out how the fire was started, and if anything else has been found at the ignition site."

Jones wrote down CAR, HOW STARTED, MOTIVES and EVIDENCE.

"So, under motives we have, insurance or fire hero."

"Fire hero?"

"Wouldn't you call it that? Someone who wants to be a hero at the scene of a fire?"

"I guess that's what you call it," said Jones. "That fits with Candace. She can swoop in and be the hero. And I suppose that's what the police are crazy enough to think about Atlas. But what about Phoenix?"

Jones shrugged. "Something to do with being in the defence force? Some after-effects of what he's seen?"

"Maybe?" said Autumn. "Or maybe whatever is going on with him was happening before he went overseas. Maybe that's what attracted him to it in the first place?"

"That's a good point," said Jones. "The perfect questions to ask Hugo, if I thought he would even answer them."

"Well, we might need to do a bit of research ourselves," said Autumn. "I wonder if there is anything online about him?"

"Let me take a look," said Jones. She pulled out her phone but the search for Phoenix and SASR showed nothing. Neither did Phoenix and Australian Soldier. "Nothing," she told Autumn.

"Interesting," said Autumn. "I guess that means he hasn't hit the news for anything, good or bad."

"Seems that way."

"Alright, let's move on. What are we going to do about the evidence portion of our investigation?" asked Autumn.

"You know exactly what we're going to have to do," said Jones, eyes lifting to rest on her sister who was smiling.

"A ghost in a police station? That plan?"

"Yep," laughed Jones. "I do feel bad, but we're going to have to try and look at the evidence file."

"I don't know how though. Won't that be in Mount Barker with the new detectives?"

Jones let out a long breath. Autumn was right. Strolling into the Lilly Pilly Creek police station and distracting Christopher wasn't going to work this time. And there was no way Jones was risking taking Autumn to Mount Barker. It was much too far. There was no way she would have enough ghost energy for that.

"Somehow, we're going to have to bring them to us," said

Autumn. Jones looked up, surprised.

"We are?"

"Yep! I'm sure we can entice them to come and speak to us if we say we have information about Atlas."

"Autumn! We can't do that!"

"What? We wouldn't tell them anything. In fact, I wouldn't mind giving them the runaround. But whilst you're banging on about a lot of irrelevant stuff, I'd take a peek at their files."

"Really? You think they're just going to open them up in front of you?"

"Well, that part is up to you!" Autumn was grinning. Jones rolled her eyes and shook her head.

The thought of sitting in front of two rather intimidating Police Detectives and intentionally manipulating them into showing Autumn their evidence, made Jones feel a little ill. And yet she couldn't bring herself to reject the idea out of hand. Unfortunately, she had to admit, Autumn's plan seemed like the only ball they had in their court.

CHAPTER 33

"It's already too late to get out!" Wren had burst into The Memory Bank.

Jones snapped her head up from the notebook to find her friend rushing across the room. She looked a little dishevelled.

"What are you talking about?"

"There's another fire and it's too late to leave," said Wren. "Can't you hear the siren?"

Jones was shocked to realise she hadn't noticed the shrill noise. It had become part of the background of Lilly Pilly Creek over the last few days, and her brain hadn't registered the sound.

"Is it close? Is it bad? What do we do?" Jones was now standing, recognising a rising panic in her chest. If the flames Autumn had seen were already threatening the town, then the fire must be moving fast.

"Jones! Can we come in here?" she turned to see Prue had rushed into the Bank, followed by three people whom Jones assumed were her real estate staff.

"Of course?" she said. "But what's going on?"

"The fire is behind the town. It's moved down the hill fast and immediately after the alert to evacuate, there was an alert to say it was too late to leave."

Jones picked up her phone and saw a list of alerts. She'd had her phone on silent. How stupid of her.

"Well, come in, make yourselves at home," said Jones. "I have a feeling there may be a few more people behind you."

She wasn't wrong. A steady stream of Lilly Pilly Creek shop owners, and a few residents, made their way into the Bank. The word had gotten out that Jones was happy to be a place of refuge. It was the largest and sturdiest building in town after all.

Jones ran around placing the damp towels at the doors and window sills, but not before unlocking the gates and turning the sprinklers on in the garden outside. She hoped it would help in some way.

Within half an hour, there was quite a gathering. Groups were forming, some having brought their own deck chairs again, others finding spaces on the ground. Everyone had their head over their phones, watching for updates from the CFS.

"Don't you think it's a bit odd Sally Butler is here?" It was Prue, who had sidled up next to Jones and nearly given her a heart attack.

"What are you talking about? Where?"

Prue pointed in the direction of a small group who were leaning up against one of the Bank's walls. "There, with the John Deer cap on. You know people are saying she deliberately lit the fire at her place," said Prue.

"No!" Jones's reaction was genuine. She had no idea the town's gossip was on the same radar as she and Autumn. Perhaps Sybil had missed this bit of information. Or not.

"Well, at least, I think it could be likely," said Prue.

"So, are there 'people' pointing the finger, or is it just you, Prue?"

"Jones, you don't know her story like I do. She's run that farm into the ground, their mortgage is through the roof, and her husband has taken on on FIFO work to make ends meet," she explained. "Just seems likely a bit of insurance money wouldn't go astray."

"You could be right," said Jones. "But that type of speculation won't lead me to kick her out of The Memory Bank."

"No, no," said Prue. "Of course not."

"But what about Rhys Bauer? Isn't he just as likely as Sally to set a fire for the insurance?"

Prue scoffed. "Not at all! He's owned that place outright for years. He might not be the best farmer in the district, but he doesn't have to." Prue leaned in closer. "Not a lot of people know, and I shouldn't be saying this, but he's quite the savvy investor. Has properties all over the place. He doesn't need insurance money."

Jones nodded in understanding. It seemed one suspect could be crossed off her list, and Sally Butler had moved to the top spot.

Prue and Jones looked sharply towards the front door as they heard fire trucks streaming past, sirens blaring. Jones looked to the high windows and noticed the orange and grey sky. Her heart was pounding, and she turned to look at everyone, wondering where Hugo was.

Despite everything, she was worried about him and decided to call. The last thing she wanted was for him to feel as though he couldn't come to the Bank.

"Excuse me, Prue," said Jones. She pulled her phone out of her pocket and made her way to a quiet corner of the Bank.

"Hugo? Are you ok? Where are you?"

"Hi Jones, I'm fine. Are you ok?"

"Yes, yes, I'm in the Bank. Half the town is here. What about you?"

"I'm coming," he said. "I thought I'd grab all the food we have, and some of the drinks, and bring them with me. Is that ok?"

"Of course," said Jones. "That's a great idea." She was relieved he had already been planning to come over.

"I saw everyone walking past the bar and knew they would be on their way. Have you got enough water?"

Jones was smiling, happy that despite their fight, Hugo was looking out for the town, for her. She glanced out at the room and knew that no, she most certainly did not have enough water.

"Right, well, I'll get the boys to bring some over with us," Hugo said. "The fellas have all been pitching in this morning. I told the rest of the staff to stay home, and I'm glad I did."

"Yes," said Jones. "It doesn't sound good out there, does it?"

"No it doesn't," said Hugo. "But don't worry, I'm sure the CFS will protect Lilly Pilly Creek."

"I hope so," said Jones, feeling her throat catch a little. Knowing Hugo was coming made her feel better, but it also meant she was now very aware of how serious the situation was.

"I won't be long," said Hugo.

"Thanks, Hugo," said Jones. "Thank you."

"Anything," said Hugo, before hanging up.

Jones turned around to see Autumn appearing through the ceiling. Jones wasn't sure how they were going to manage to communicate with all of these people around. It was crowded and no doubt someone would notice if Jones huddled in a corner talking to herself.

Fortunately Autumn appeared to read her mind.

"Meet me in the tower," she called.

Jones nodded as her sister floated directly up the centre of the staircase. Without drawing attention to herself, Jones made her way over to the stairs and climbed slowly up. She still didn't visit the tower very often. It was the scene of two of the worst days of her life. However, Jones couldn't help but smile, because it had been Hugo who had rescued her, pinning Jamie Royce to a wall so Jones could escape his grasp.

"Is it bad?" Jones asked as she entered the tower room.

"Yep," said Autumn. "If you look out the window you can see the flames just behind Main Street. It's on our doorstep."

"Oh my god," said Jones. "Do you think we're safe? Will the Bank keep us safe?"

"I'm not sure about the Bank, but look at all those trucks and all that water. If anyone is going to keep us safe, it's the CFS."

Jones stood on her tiptoes, pushing herself up on the window sill and saw spouts of water attacking the flames, women and men in their orange uniforms and helmets forming a wall between Lilly Pilly Creek and the fire. These brave people were the only thing standing in the way of this fire wiping out Lilly Pilly Creek. In that moment, Jones thought of her family, the ones who had passed, but not returned as ghosts, and willed them to help the firefighters protect the town they loved.

"I wish there was something we could do to help?" said Jones, turning back to Autumn.

"There's nothing we can do," said Autumn. "Not right now. After all of this has settled down, that will be when we can help the most. For now, we just need to keep everyone safe and calm."

Jones nodded and glanced back out the window.

"I almost forgot," said Jones. "Prue just told me some very interesting information."

"Oh?"

"She said that Rhys Bauer has no reason to seek insurance money. He's loaded by the sounds of it. But Sally Butler is another story."

"Really," Autumn said, her mouth wide.

"They're struggling, the farm, their mortgage, and Prue wouldn't put it past her to set a fire for the insurance."

"Gosh!" said Autumn. "Do you think she's told this to the police?"

"I've got no idea," said Jones. "But if it was her, do you think she set the Rhys Bauer fire too?"

Autumn shrugged. "Who knows? If she was cunning enough, she might have planned the whole thing, and realised it was better to light the decoy fire first."

"Gosh, I just don't know what to think," said Jones. "And with the fire literally on our doorstep, I can't seem to think straight."

"I'm going to head out to take another look," said Autumn.

"What?" Jones shot a look of surprise at her sister. "Is that safe?"

Autumn smiled. "Of course, I'm dead remember."

"I know," said Jones. "But surely the fire does something to you, to your energy or something?"

Autumn shook her head. "Nope. Nothing. I can glide right

through it. You remember the candle?"

"Yes, but that was a tiny candle flame. This is a ranging bush fire!"

"I'm fine Jones," said Autumn. "You can't even imagine what it feels like for me."

Jones sighed. No, she most certainly could not. The idea of her sister, even though she was already dead, literally floating into a bushfire, made her feel ill.

"Jones! Are you up here?"

Jones's heart leapt. Hugo. He appeared at the top of the staircase.

"I'll leave you to it," said Autumn, gliding through the wall and out into the hot, windy and raging world outside.

"Hugo," said Jones, and without thinking, she walked over and hugged him.

"Are you ok?" he asked.

"I'm fine," said Jones. "Just a little overwhelmed and scared. Take a look out the window."

Jones pulled away and let Hugo take in the view she had just been privy to.

"It's a hell of a lot closer than I realised," said Hugo. "Maybe we shouldn't be here?" He turned back to face Jones.

"It's too late," said Jones, feeling her voice quiver. "They won't let us out. We have to stay. But surely the Bank will keep us safe?"

Hugo walked over and took her hands. "We will be safe. We'll keep everyone down there safe, and I know the CFS are going to protect Lilly Pilly Creek." Taking her hands, he lifted them to his lips and kissed them. "Shall we head down?'

Jones smiled and nodded. She very much hoped Hugo was right.

CHAPTER 34

"Jones!" Prue was calling to her as she descended back into the main area. "Sergeant Schmidt is here to see you!"

Prue was right. There was Christopher, in full Sergeant uniform, with one of his officers next to him.

"How can I help?" asked Jones, walking up to Christopher. Prue was hovering, clearly trying to make herself a part of whatever he was doing there.

Christopher tilted his head, motioning for the two of them to step away from the crowd. Jones lead him in the direction of the lockbox room. They didn't go inside, but it was suitably far enough away that no one should overhear as long as they weren't intentionally eavesdropping.

"That fire looks pretty bad out there," said Jones.

"Oh, have you been outside?"

"No," Jones shook her head. "I was just looking from the tower. There's a pretty good vantage point. It doesn't look good. So close."

"I've just been speaking to Candace, and she seems to think if they can hold it off for another few hours, then the wind is supposed to die down, and possibly even a bit of rain."

"Really? Thank goodness." Jones felt her shoulders drop, not realising until that moment how tense she had been.

"That's what she said," said Christopher.

"And what started it? Do they know yet?"

Christopher glanced around, noticing his Officer hadn't followed them. Jones was surprised to see Autumn had returned and was peering at the officer's folder. She was trying to get a look at the file notes.

"Arson, again," Christopher whispered.

Jones's eyes went wide. "Seriously? A completely new fire?"

He nodded. "It seems like they wanted it to look like a flare up but it was most certainly deliberately lit."

"But how? Christopher, do you know what they're using?" asked Jones. "Do you know how they're fighting the fires?"

Christopher took a deep breath. "Jones, I can't really tell you. I shouldn't tell you. But look, you simply cannot tell anyone. Not Hugo. Not Sybil. No one."

Jones nodded seriously. "I promise."

"Mosquito coils."

"What?" Jones's mind immediately went to the green spirals that people often lit and put out at barbeques to keep the mozzies away.

Christopher nodded. "Quite clever really, but they've forgotten that there is usually a small metal tab at the very end. It's taken the arson investigators a while to work it out. But they had a suspicion yesterday, so it was pretty obvious when they took a look this morning. Same again."

Jones shook her head. Knowing how these fires were lit, that they were in fact deliberate, suddenly hit her.

"And I bet they're pointing the finger at Atlas again, right?"

"I'm afraid to say, yes."

"They're unbelievable," said Jones. "You've obviously told them there is no way Atlas is responsible for this!"

"Of course I have," said Christopher. "And to be honest, it sounds like he has an alibi for today's fire, but they aren't listening."

"An alibi?"

"He says he hasn't left home for days," said the Sergeant. "But they're saying he could have snuck out early this morning, lit the fire, and come back before anyone noticed him gone."

"Honestly! That's their story! Are they even looking at anyone else?"

"Well that's the thing," said Christopher, glancing around before continuing. "And look, you know of course I shouldn't be telling you any of this."

"Yes, of course," said Jone. "But if they're not going to listen, then *someone* has to help Altas."

"Exactly," said Christopher. "So, at the last two fires, people have noticed a car that was similar to Atlas's. But not this time."

"So, no cars were seen?"

"Nope," said Jones. "Not one recalls anything except fire trucks and all the media that seem to have descended on Lilly Pilly Creek."

"Yes, well that's to be expected," said Jones.

"Yep," said Christopher. "Repeat arson events and the fact that this fire is threatening the town has the media in a tizzy. They're all over the place, trying to get past roadblocks. It's a nightmare."

"I suppose they're only trying to do their job," said Jones, completely understanding what the newsrooms would be expecting from the journalists.

"Yes, yes, of course," said Christopher, his face showing he recognised his mistake. "But I still have to do mine, and that means keeping them, and this town safe. For now, I think they're out of the way. But do you have any ideas? Any thoughts about who you think might be doing this? Have you heard anything?"

"You're asking me?" Jones said.

"Come on, no need for pretence," said Christopher. "I know you'd be investigating. At least trying to work out what's going on for Atlas's sake. So, what do you have for me?"

Jones glanced around. Autumn was nowhere to be seen. She desperately wanted her nod of approval, to agree that it was ok to share their thoughts. But she wasn't there. Jones would have to trust her gut on this one, and it was telling her to do anything to protect Atlas. Even if it meant Hugo would despise her.

"Ok ok," said Jones. "Well, it's not much. I mean, I'm sure the farmers whose land the fires started on have been looked at. You know, insurance as the motive."

Christopher nodded, confirming her suspicions.

"Right, well then there's also other members of the CFS to look at. Just because Atlas is the newest member doesn't mean some other firefighter isn't to blame. Could be someone from another crew. Could even be Candace."

"Candace?" said Christopher. "What makes you say that?"

"Oh, no one specific reason. Just that she is a firefighter, and she was pretty quick to point the finger at Atlas. Could be she is deflecting blame?"

"Ok, well, I know Candace pretty well so I wouldn't think it was her. But sure, I'll consider it. Anything else?"

"Well, there is one other person," said Jones. "And I hate to say it, but there's just a few things that seem, well, suspicious."

"Hit me," said Christopher.

"So, don't look, but you know Hugo has three friends visiting at the moment," said Jones.

Christopher nodded.

"Ok, well, the quiet one, with the black hair. Up until yesterday, he was always carrying around a lighter, flicking it constantly. I think it's a nervous habit. You see, um, well, he has been in the Defence Forces, and I don't know, maybe he has some PTSD? That combined with the lighter? I don't know. It just seems worth looking into."

"You're right, that does sound very interesting," said Christopher. "What's his name?"

"Phoenix," Jones whispered, leaning in. "Sorry, I don't know his last name."

"And how does Hugo know him?" asked Christopher.

"Ah, um, you might have to ask Phoenix that," said Jones. "But you won't confront him straight away, will you? You'll investigate first, right? I mean I could be way off beam, and well, it's just…." Jones couldn't finish the sentence.

"If I start asking questions, Hugo will know who told me?" Christopher raised his eyebrows.

Jones looked at her feet. "Exactly."

"Don't worry, Jones," he said, pulling out his notebook to write down everything she had to say. "I won't speak to him unless I have reason to."

"Are we safe?"

"What, from the arsonist?"

"No, I mean in the Bank. Are we safe? Will we be ok?"

"Jones, I think you are as safe as you can be in Lilly Pilly Creek. The only people safer are those who thought to leave last night or early this morning. And you were never going to do that, were you?"

Jones tilted her head slightly, a cheeky smile on her face. "Never."

There were suddenly a few shouts and squeals in the room. The power had gone out.

"Oh, that doesn't seem good," said Jones.

"They've more than likely turned the power off for safety," said Christopher. "Or a powerline has been brought down. It will be fine."

As Jones turned to face the darkened room, now only lit by the murky orange sky outside, she truly hoped he was right.

CHAPTER 35

"Jones, there you are." It was Hugo.

"Of course, I'm here," said Jones. "Where have you been?" She realised she hadn't seen him since he first arrived.

"I've been helping Sybil. We brought her van into the garden," said Hugo. "We thought it would be easier and safer there. We've put some of the food and drinks in there. Rex said your generator wasn't working, but Sybil does have a small one which could prove handy now," he said, looking up a the lights which no longer glowed. "I hope that's ok?"

Jones was a little taken aback by his last question. Of course it was ok, it was a great idea. But she realised he too may still be feeling a little sensitive about their fight. Did she need to mention it? If she was honest with herself, she was not feeling ready to have that conversation. For now, she would pretend everything was fine, and hoped he would continue doing the same!

"I think it's a great idea!" She beamed at him. "But I thought Sybil was planning on leaving?"

"Too late," said Hugo. "I think the speed of this fire has taken everyone by surprise."

Jones shook her head. "Is there anything I can do to help?"

Hugo hesitated. "Do you think you might be able to help me bring the bags of ice in? I thought we could maybe fill the bathroom basins with ice, for drinks or whatever we need," he explained.

"Sure. But where are the guys?" Jones asked, looking around the room. "I thought they were helping you?"

"They were," said Hugo. "But they put their name down with BlazeAid to help with rebuilding fences and they just got the call-up."

"Blazeaid?" asked Jones.

"They help with rebuilding after fires," said Hugo. "They won't do much until everything has calmed down, but one of the properties needs help with temporary fencing for their stock so that's what they're doing."

"Poor blokes," said Jones shaking her head. "It's boiling out there."

Hugo grinned. "Nothing those guys can't handle." Jones smiled, knowing she had no understanding of what the conditions would have been like in Afghanistan. Hopefully one day Hugo would speak to her about it.

"Oh my gosh," Jones had turned to stare at the entrance of the Memory Bank, the door open wide.

It was Atlas.

Jones didn't say a word. She just ran over and scooped him up into a long hug. After a second, his arms wrapped around her, and she recognised a feeling of tension and desperation in them. They stood there for a while, Jones fighting back tears, and Atlas breathing in and out deeply, until he seemed to calm a little. Autumn floated next to her sister, sadly watching Atlas.

"Atlas, are you ok?" Jones asked, stepping back slightly but still gripping his upper arms.

"I'm ok," said Atlas. "For now. Who knows what they'll pull together to frame me."

"Oh Atlas, don't speak like that."

Jones glanced around to see a group of people hovering, just in hearing distance.

"Well, it's true," said Atlas, scowling.

"It does seem that way," said Jones.

Wren walked up next to them. "Have you been in touch with Adam? He's Atlas's new lawyer," Wren explained to Jones.

Atlas nodded. "Thanks, Wren. Yes, he's been excellent. He's the reason I'm standing here and not stuck in one of their cells again."

"I did my best," said Wren.

"Oh no Wren, you were amazing. You did everything you could. Today was a very different day. They had no evidence to hold me. Not even a fanciful sighting of my car. No, it was an easier ride for Adam today. But gee the way he spoke to them, it was a joy to behold." Atlas managed to let out a laugh, and Wren and Jones joined in.

Jones was relieved to hear Atlas was in very good hands.

"But enough about me," said Atlas. "Seeing as I can't be out there fighting the fires, I want to be of some use. How can I help?"

It was Sybil who stepped up. "Any chance you want to help me make some sandwiches?" she asked, walking from where she and Prue had been hovering. "I'm setting up a bit of a production line in that back office and another set of hands would be a lifesaver."

"At your service!" said Atlas and he strode off towards the sandwich-making station.

Jones looked at Sybil who winked before following him. Jones realised Sybil was perfectly capable of making the sandwiches but knew how important it was to keep Atlas busy today.

"What's going to happen?" Jones turned and asked Wren.

Before Wren had a chance to answer, Prue was at their side. "Is it true? The police think Atlas is the arsonist?"

Jones looked at Wren, who took the lead. "Prue, you know we can't say anything."

"Okay, okay," said Prue. "But hypothetically, if anyone was accusing someone in this building, for example, a young male in his 20s, would it be smart to have him stay?"

"What are you trying to say, Prue?" Jones said, louder than she meant. "A few minutes ago you were the one doing the accusing."

"And Sally Butler is no longer here."

"Prue! What did you do!"

"Nothing, nothing," she said. "She left at the same time that group of gorgeous burly men left."

Jones rolled her eyes but realised it must have been Sally's property the blokes were going to work at.

"Come on Jones," said Prue. "I know Atlas has done a lot for you. But seriously, it's not safe to have a potential arsonist in here, is it? Can you imagine if this whole place were to go up in smoke? What would that do to you? To your business?"

"Prue," Wren said, shaking her head. "You are walking on thin ice. If you say another word against someone very important to Jones, to this town, then I am going to have to ask you to leave."

"What? You'd throw us out into the street in the middle of a bushfire?"

"Well, haven't you just been saying it isn't safe here in The Memory Bank?"

"Wren, you know that's not what I meant?" Prue's eyes blazed.

"Do I? If I was you, I'd go and find a seat and keep my trap shut."

Wren and Jones stared at Prue, frowning and crossing their arms.

"Fine, if that's how you want to be. But when everything hits the fan, don't come running to me for help."

Prue spun on her heel and made her way back to her team who had set themselves up around one of the customer tables. She ingratiated herself back into the group with humour, saying something and laughing loudly, with the rest of them politely following.

"Gosh, I really would like to throw her out," said Jones.

"I thought she was getting better," said Wren. "But she's just the same. Only thinking of herself."

"Impossible," said Jones. "In the meantime, I'm meant to be helping Hugo with the ice."

Jones made her way to the garden doors, but Autumn caught her just before she could turn the handle.

"I couldn't see anything," said Autumn.

"In the file?"

Autumn nodded. "She did flick through some things once. The page she was on seemed to be a timeline but I didn't get a good enough look before she closed it again. Sorry."

"No need to apologise," said Jones. "We'll just have to rely on something else to prove Atlas's innocence."

"I hope we find it," said Autumn.

Jones nodded and looked out the glass doors. She could see Hugo with a shirt wrapped around his mouth. It was windy, smoky, and no doubt a furnace out there. She slipped off the button-up shirt she had on over her t-shirt, and wrapped it around her mouth and nose, before venturing out.

The thing that shocked her the most as she opened the door and stepped outside was the noise. There was a violent whooshing and crackling sound like nothing she had ever heard before.

"Hugo! I'm here to help!" she jogged over to help, shielding her eyes from the ash that was darting about in the air.

"Jones! What are you doing out here?" Hugo yelled above the roar around them.

"The ice! I'm helping with the ice!"

"Go back in! I've taken it to the bathroom!"

"What are *you* doing then?"

"Just grabbing a few last things! Get back inside. The smoke. It isn't safe."

Jones wanted to say the same to him, but she knew he wouldn't be long, and if she was honest, she didn't want to spend another second outside.

"Ooof," she groaned, pushing the door closed against the firestorm. Untying the shirt from her mouth, she scrunched it into a ball as she made her way to the bathroom. Hugo had laid the ice bags in two of the basins. Jones found the plugs and then started emptying ice into them. They were lovely, old-fashioned basins, deep and wide. They would hold quite a few drinks and anything else that needed to be kept cool. She kept one free for handwashing but the other two were ready.

"It's awful out there," said Hugo, carrying in a crate of plastic water bottles.

Jones bent down to grab some. "I know. It's right on our doorstep, isn't it? I can't imagine being a firefighter."

"I guess they have all the right gear, but still."

"Yep! To be honest, despite everything, I'm kind of glad Atlas is safe and sound in here. I wouldn't say that to him of course."

"Well, I'd like to know who's responsible for this whole mess. Atlas, the fires. Putting the town in danger."

Jones looked at him but didn't say anything.

"Now, come on, you can't still think Phoenix has anything to do with it." Hugo's eyes flashed black, arms folded across his chest.

"Look, if you don't believe he has anything to do with it, then no," said Jones, sighing. "It's the same with me and Atlas. There's no way he could have done it, despite all the finger-pointing in his direction."

"Exactly," said Hugo. "And hopefully no one has been pointing fingers in the direction of Phoenix."

Jones busied herself with the water bottles, not wanting to catch Hugo's eye. "Well, Christopher may question him."

"What!"

Jones glanced up and then continued with the water bottles. "Well, he was asking about everyone. Asking if there was anyone new in town. Anyone I suspected."

"And of course you said Phoenix! How could you?"

"Look Hugo, I know he's your friend, and he likely hasn't done anything."

"Likely! So you do still think he's involved."

"This is to protect Atlas!" Jones said loudly. "We need to police looking somewhere other than him. And Phoenix isn't the only name I gave. First of all, I think this Candace woman a a much stronger candidate than Phoenix. And Sally Butler for that matter."

Jones caught movement out the side of her eye and saw Autumn glide in, raising her eyebrows.

"But you still had Phoenix on your list!" Hugo retorted.

"He walks around with a lighter for goodness sake," Autumn said.

"He was last! Last on this list! But I'm trying to help Atlas," Jones heard her voice crack, and tears started to well. "That's all I'm trying to do. They're not looking at anyone else and if we don't help, Atlas's life might be ruined forever."

"I hope you're not fighting about me?"

Hugo, Jones and Autumn turned to see Atlas standing in the doorway.

CHAPTER 36

"Sorry Atlas," said Jones. She wiped her hands on her shorts. "We're ok, we're just trying to help."

"Thanks, Jones," said Atlas. "But I don't think accusing Hugo's friends is going to help."

Jones found she had tears running down her cheeks. She looked up at Hugo. "I know, I'm so sorry. Atlas is right. Phoenix is a friend of yours, and if you believe he isn't involved, then I believe you."

Hugo nodded, Jones unsure if he was accepting her apology but at least he was listening to her.

"But who is it? Who the hell is lighting fires around Lilly Pilly Creek and putting us all at risk? If the police can't work it out, then we have to. Somehow!"

"Maybe I can help?" said Atlas. "The police dropped some information whilst they were trying to interrogate me today." Atlas couldn't help but roll his eyes.

"Oh really! Like what?"

"Perhaps we shouldn't keep talking here in the bathroom," said Hugo, glancing around and shrugging his shoulders.

"Yes, yes good point," said Jones. "Shall we go into the lockbox room? Grab some chairs. And maybe ask Wren to join us?"

Hugo nodded. "Sounds good. I'll bring some drinks in. Atlas how were the sandwiches going?"

"All done," said Atlas. "I'll grab some and we'll meet you there."

As Jones rounded up Wren and pulled some extra chairs into the lockbox room, she was reminded of the first case they had all worked on, when they had invited Clancy to The Memory Bank to find out what he knew about Autumn's death. Jones had only just met Hugo then, but very quickly he had become a part of their lives. Her life. Now, she realised, she was a risk of pushing him away completely. She had to trust him. Just as she expected him to trust her. The fear of something happening to Atlas couldn't dictate how she treated those around her. She was just going to have to forget about Phoenix. If Hugo was right, then they would waste too much time barking up the wrong tree. They needed to focus on the evidence, and hopefully, Atlas had more to share with them.

"Gosh I love an egg salad sandwich," said Wren, her mouth full of wholemeal bread, egg, mayonnaise and iceberg lettuce, when Jones sat down next to her.

Jones had to say she was also enjoying the sandwiches, having picked up one containing corned beef and sweet mustard pickles.

Hugo was also working his way through a variety of sandwiches, but Atlas, Jones noted, had one piece on the plate in front of him and it hadn't been touched.

Jones glanced out the room's windows and saw Prue watching them. She had tried to wheedle her way in, but Wren had cleverly played the lawyer card and gave some spiel about confidentiality and Atlas's best interest and other things Jones didn't understand, and she presumed Prue didn't either. Bottom line, Atlas didn't want her there and that was that.

"Right," Jones said, putting her half-eaten triangle down, and picking up her pen. "Let's get to work."

Hugo nodded, wiping crumbs off his hands, and taking a swig from the iced coffee next to him. Wren grabbed another egg sandwich, and Autumn positioned herself high on the window sill. All their eyes turned to Atlas.

"What do you want to know?" he asked.

"First of all Atlas," said Wren. "I do want to make it clear that you don't have to tell us anything. It's entirely up to you and your lawyer. So please, I hope you don't feel pressured by us."

Atlas smiled and nodded. "It's fine," he said. "I need all the help I can get and we know this group's track record. I could do a heck of a lot worse than to have all of you on my side, trying to work this out."

Jones reached out and squeezed Atlas's forearm.

"So, why did the cops let you go this morning?" Hugo asked.

"Because they had no evidence," said Atlas. "They were trying to get me to trip up. But I couldn't because, like I told them over and over, I hadn't left home in days. And no, I didn't sneak out early this morning, light a fire, and get back in bed before anyone in my house noticed. Does he have any idea what time my Grandma gets up!"

The group laughed at this. They could all relate to the early hours grandparents seemed to wake.

"Every other time they've said that a car like yours was spotted," said Jones. "But that wasn't the case today?"

Atlas shook his head. "Nope. The only people that anyone had seen were the firies, the police, the news folk, and Blazeaid.

"So, no motorbike?" Hugo asked, daring to raise his eyebrows in

Jones's direction.

"Motorbike? Nup. No mention of a motorbike."

Hugo winked at Jones, and she managed a small smile. She hoped their exchange of words earlier was just in the heat of the moment, and they were back on the same team.

"But they're adamant a car like yours was seen near the first two ignition points?" said Wren.

"Yep, they went on and on about it," said Atlas. "So unless it was all made up, there must be someone out there with a car like mine."

"Can you describe your car?" asked Jones, her journalist pen poised.

"It's a Toyota Corolla. A four-door hatchback," he said.

Hugo had his phone out, searching. "What colour? Blue?"

"Yep," he said. "They call it Blue Gem. Yes, the police have gone into that much detail."

"Gosh," Jones shook her head. "They're serious."

"So, we've got to find out who else has a similar-looking car," said Hugo, holding out his phone to show the group.

Jones gasped, but Autumn was the only one who noticed.

"What?" Autumn flew down from her perch and took up position at Jones's side.

There was a knock on the door.

"Christopher!" said Jones, standing abruptly. She pulled the door open and invited him in, surprised that he had returned so quickly.

"Sergeant Schmidt," said Wren. "Anything we can help with?"

He turned and pulled the door closed before speaking.

"Yes there is," he said. "But no one can know I'm speaking to you." He glanced at Atlas. "And I'm also going to pretend Atlas isn't here. Right?"

Everyone nodded vigorously.

"Of course," said Jones. "Shall I grab you a seat?"

Christopher shook his head. "No, I'm right. This won't take long. What are you all doing in here, by the way?"

"Trying to solve the crime!" Autumn cried out. Jones tried to keep her face straight, as she happened to catch Atlas's eye. He frowned a little but then turned back to Christopher.

"We're trying to save Atlas," said Wren.

"Thought that might be the case," he replied. "So am I. I wanted to give you an update. I've got some alibis."

Jones couldn't help but smile. Despite risking his job, Christopher was going to do whatever it took to save Atlas.

"Lay it on us," said Hugo.

"Right, well, Candace is airtight. She's been on meetings and calls most of the night, and has barely slept. So we can account for basically every minute of her night and early this morning."

"The captain?" asked Atlas. "You thought she was the arsonist?"

"Had to chase every lead," Christopher responded. "Next one was Rhys…. He's been in Adelaide for the last few days. Not planning on coming back until everything calms down. So that takes him off the list.'

"So who does that leave, on your list?" Hugo asked, a sideways glance at Jones. She raised her eyebrows but kept her eyes on her hands in her lap.

"We have Sally Butler and," Christopher paused to look at Hugo. "Well, your mate actually. Phoenix."

"Of course you do," said Hugo, his voice not hiding his disdain. "Any alibi's for him?"

"Well, no, not yet. But I'm about to head out to Sally's farm to speak to him."

"Phoenix is at Sally Butler's farm?" Wren looked confused.

"Yep," said Hugo. "He and the fella's are out there helping with the fences. But I know that Phoenix has an alibi. He was in his swag at my place."

"Was he?" asked Christopher. "And you can account for his whereabouts for the whole night?"

"Well, we were all asleep for most of it," said Hugo. "But I would have heard if his motorbike started up."

Christopher nodded. "Fair enough," he said. "You're probably right. But I'd still like to talk to him. And I need to see if Sally has an alibi. So I'm going to head out there now. Anything else you think I should know?"

Autumn glanced at Jones, but she didn't say a word. Everyone else shook their heads.

"Well, if you think of anything, give me a call." Christopher left the room.

"Hugo," said Jones. "Can I take a look at that car again?"

Hugo handed his phone to Jones. She looked at it, and her stomach sank.

"Jones! Who is it? Who do you think is the arsonist?" said Autumn.

Jones caught Autumn's eye and frowned. She wasn't going to say anything. Not until she was sure.

"I have a feeling the fellas are going to need some help," said Hugo.

"What do you mean?" asked Wren.

"With Phoenix. I wish I was out there, you know, to back them up. I bet Phoenix freezes and won't say anything. And the other two, well I imagine they're going to get pretty snarky with Christopher and stuff everything up."

"But you can't go," said Jones. "It's too dangerous."

"The fire's heading in the other direction," said Hugo. "As long as no one stops me, I reckon I can get there. I'll just tell them I'm helping Blazeaid too.'

"Well I'm coming too!" said Jones.

"It's too dangerous," said Hugo.

Jones shook her head. "If you're going, I'm going."

"And I'm going too!" said Atlas. "One way or another, it seems the arsonist is going to be there, and I want to look them in the eye."

"Sounds like we're all heading out there," said Wren, raising her eyebrows.

Jones heard Autumn laugh. But she didn't crack a smile.

CHAPTER 37

"We'll take my ute," said Hugo. "That should be the safest if we have to go on any rough roads."

"Can we all fit?" asked Atlas.

"Sure can!"

Before they walked out the door Jones went and quickly whispered to Sybil, letting her know they were investigating, but not to tell anyone.

"Maybe just say we're popping out for supplies," said Jones. "Hopefully that will keep Prue in line."

They both knew Prue was going to be the biggest nosy parker out of the now substantial group of townsfolk who were finding refuge from the fire.

"Sure thing," said Sybil.

Jones handed Sybil her key. "Just in case you need to leave," she explained. "Thanks, Sybil. I know I can count on you to look after everyone. And the Bank."

Jones wanted desperately to hug her but knew that would only raise suspicion, so she quickly said goodbye, and, wrapping her shirt once again over her nose and mouth, ventured outside.

Hugo had pulled the dual cab ute right up to the front of the Bank. There, relaxing casually in the tray, was Autumn. Jones couldn't help but laugh before she jumped into the back seat next to Wren.

"All set?" Hugo turned his head slightly, checking everyone was buckled in.

"Let's do this!" said Jones.

Although Jones knew Hugo wanted to drive flat chat, it was impossible to go very fast. The smoke was thick, and even with the headlights on it was impossible to see very far in front. However, Christopher was no doubt having to take things at a snail's pace also, so they shouldn't be too far away from him.

Gradually, as they drove further on, the smoke reduced and their sight improved. It also meant they could see more clearly the blackened gum trees, melted water tanks and red flames still flickering in burnt-out stumps as they drove by.

None of them spoke. It was the first time they had seen the devastation first-hand. The importance of catching this arsonist suddenly weighed very heavily on Jones. This was no ordinary case. This was the hunt for someone who appeared to have no care for the people around them. No concept of how much danger they were putting so many people in. It was impossible to fathom how someone could do this.

Jones watched the blue dot of their car slowly move along the ute's navigation screen showing the route to Sally's farm. Only a few more minutes until they got there. She had no idea what to expect. What to say? And if her suspicions were correct. She would have to play things very close to her chest.

It was at that moment that Autumn decided to poke her head through the back window, making Jones jump.

"Alright back there?" Hugo called, as Wren looked at her strangely.

"Yep, sorry, don't know what came over me," Jones laughed it off but desperately wanted to glare at her sister.

"Come on Jones, give me a clue," Autumn hissed. "Who do you think it is?"

Jones of course couldn't answer her, so she had no idea what Autumn was thinking, questioning her at this moment. Perhaps she was feeling lonely in the back. Jones was so anxious she hadn't even questioned whether Autumn was travelling too far from The Memory Bank.

As they turned onto the dirt road to Sally's farm, it became evident they wouldn't have long before they found the fencing crew. They saw crisp black droppers and shiny wire mesh forming a fence that had only been recently hung. A ute and three motorbikes were pulled off to the side.

They continued following the road until, up in the distance, they spotted Christopher's police car pulled up alongside a four-wheel drive.

"He's talking to the fellas," said Hugo, quickly pulling over and then jumping out of the ute. The three passengers and Autumn quickly followed. Jones realised she wasn't wearing the best footwear to tackle uneven and burnt scrubland.

"Hugo! What are you doing here?" It was Christopher who had turned to watch the group lumber over to him.

"Just here to support my mate, Phoenix," Hugo said, slapping Phoenix on the back.

"It's ok Hugo," said Phoenix. "Just a mix-up. All sorted."

Hugo looked at him, at Phoenix, and then back at Christopher. "Is that right? All sorted?"

Christopher nodded. "Yep, it sure is," he said. "But I have someone else I need to speak to." He cocked his head in the direction of a woman who was whacking a dropper into the ground with a large mallet. Sally looked tough and strong as she slammed the metal into the ground. Maybe she *was* capable of lighting a bushfire? Glancing at Autumn, Jones tilted her head, suggesting Autumn follow Christopher, and she quickly flew away.

Jones stood, looking around for Rusty and Chappy. She turned in the other direction and made a small squeal. She hadn't realised whose vehicle the four-wheel drive was, as it was parked on the other side of the police car.

"What's wrong Jones?" asked Hugo, walking over to her.

"Oh gosh," said Jones, her head in her hands.

"Jones! What is it?" asked Wren.

"I'm not entirely sure." Jones was shaking her head, trying to work out what to do. She turned around again, finally spotting Rusty and Chappy, talking with someone further down the tree line.

The group were staring at her, silent.

"Jones?" asked Hugo. "What's going on?

"Look, just follow my lead," said Jones. She took a deep breath, and ignoring the sticks scratching at her bare legs, Jones strode in the direction of Hugo's friends.

"Jones!" The third person with Rusty and Chappy was calling out, waving.

It was Quinn.

"I'm just interviewing these two volunteers for tomorrow's cover story."

"Oh, another cover?" Jones asked, forcing a smile.

"Well, at least I hope so," Quinn replied.

"I hope she's not asking too many tricky questions," Jones said to Rusty.

"Nah, not at all," he laughed. "A breeze. I do like to rabbit on."

"That you do," Hugo smiled, standing close to Jones.

"I wondered if I might be able to ask a question of my own," said Jones.

"Go right ahead," said Quinn, waving her hand towards the men.

"Oh no, actually Quinn, my question is for you."

"It is?"

Jones noticed Atlas and Wren look at her, questioningly. She felt Hugo place his hand on the small of her back, as though he had worked out what she was doing.

"Yes Quinn," said Jones. "It's a bit silly really. But I thought you'd be the one who'd know."

"Sure! What is it?" Quinn beamed, pleased that Jones was seeking her advice.

"Just these roads are all pretty torn up after the fire," said Jones. "And I imagine they are going to be for a while. We came here in Hugo's ute, but now I'm wondering, am I going to be alright trying to drive my Mini around on these roads?"

Quinn shrugged and frowned. "Oh, um, I'm not sure. I'm in the work four-wheel drive, so I can't compare it."

"But you've only had the work four-wheel drive today, haven't you?"

"Oh, my god," Jones heard Autumn say.

"Ah yes," said Quinn. "Remember, Jock let me take it," she said, raising her eyebrows.

"But before that, you were driving around in your car, weren't you?" said Jones. "That's a lot smaller right?"

Quinn frowned, but before she could answer, they heard Christopher, yelling. What was going on?

The group turned to see him running towards them and waving frantically.

"What the hell?" Hugo said.

"Get back in the car!" Christopher yelled.

The group were confused. What was going on?

"What!" Wren yelled back.

"Get back in the car! There's been a flare up and it's heading straight up the hill behind us!"

"Oh no!" cried out Atlas. "Quick everyone!"

"Stop!" shouted Jones, turning back to face Quinn. "Not before she answers the question."

"What question? Come on Jones. We have to go," said Wren, grabbing at Jones's arm.

"The question about her car," said Jones.

"Oh," said Atlas, appearing to catch on, pausing before turning to face Quinn. "Her car."

"Quinn, you have been driving your own car around the last few days, haven't you?'

"Ah, yes, of course," she said, pulling the clipboard she was holding protectively up to her chest.

"And remind me again, your car is a Mazda? A Kia?"

"A Hyundai," she said, not sounding as confident as she had previously.

They could hear Christopher still calling out, getting closer and closer, but Jones kept going.

"Yes, that's it. A little Hyundai hatchback, isn't it?"

Quinn nodded.

"And what colour is it again? Purple?"

"Purple? No, no it's blue."

"You're joking!" cried out Wren.

"So, it's blue? So what?" Quinn sounded defensive now.

"You bloody well know what!" cried Atlas. "It was you! You're the arsonist!"

Quinn's mouth opened, and her face went pale, dropping her clipboard. Then she started running. Running as fast as she could back to her car. Atlas took off, racing after her, the two of them stumbling, Atlas shouting.

"What the hell is going on?"Christopher said as he arrived, puffing, hands on hips, trying to find enough air.

"It's Quinn!" said Jones. "Quinn's the arsonist!"

"What?"

"It's her! She has the little blue car," said Jones. "Go! Go arrest her!"

"But she's got a four-wheel drive," Christopher said, still puffing and looking very confused.

"It's her!" Wren cried out. "Go nab her! We'll explain later."

They all turned in the direction of Quinn and Atlas, but they could no longer see them.

"Where are they?" Hugo asked.

"I'll go," said Autumn, flying away.

Wren, Hugo, Jones and Christopher all started running. Jones assumed they were struggling on the other side of Quinn's car, but when they got there, the driver's door was open, but neither of them could be seen.

"They've run off," said Jones. "But which way?" Then she shouted again. "Which direction?" It was Autumn she was calling to.

She heard her sister yell back. "Straight into the path of the fire!"

CHAPTER 38

"Oh no," said Jones. "I think they've gone the wrong way. I think they're heading towards the fire."

"What makes you say that?" said Hugo.

"It's just a feeling I have," said Jones, before spinning around. "And I can't see them anywhere else.

Phoenix, Rusy and Chappy came rushing over.

"What's going on?" asked Phoenix.

Hugo quickly explained to them, as Jones jumped into the driver's seat of his ute. She shut the door and started the engine before anyone else noticed.

"Jones!" she heard everyone call out, but she ignored them. She was going after Atlas. After everything he had gone through, she wasn't going to let the flames get him now.

She didn't drive fast, just fast enough that anyone on foot behind her couldn't keep up. She also didn't want to run down Quinn and Atlas. The smoke was starting to build, and it was getting harder and harder to see. She kept waiting for Autumn to appear, to tell her where to go, what to do.

"Maybe if I wind down the window, I'll hear her," Jones thought. The smoke swirled in, and she pulled her arm across her nose and mouth, trying to stop from breathing in the smoke, driving one-handed.

She glanced out her rearview mirror, knowing Christopher would be following her, but the smoke blocked any vision either of them might have.

The crunching of tyres over branches and rocks was downing out any other noises. Jones decided to risk it and stop driving for a moment, to see if she could hear anything.

For a few moments, all she could hear was her own rapid breathing. She took a deep breath and held it for a moment, willing her ears to pick up any sound that might help her. Nothing. Slowly, slowly she rolled further before stopping again. This time she poked her head out of the car window in an attempt to hear better. She was hit with a face full of ash. Still nothing. And then she heard her.

"Atlas! Atlas, turn to your left! Your left!"

It was Autumn. She was with him. She was guiding him away from the fire.

"That's it! Keep going!"

But he wouldn't be able to hear her? How could she possibly help him? Atlas needed the two of them working together.

Jones put the car in park, leaving it idle in anticipation of a quick getaway, and got out of the car.

"Atlas! It's Jones! Can you hear me?" She yelled but felt as though her voice was muffled by the smoke.

"Leave it to me!" Jones heard her sister's voice. "It's going to be ok."

Jones stopped. "But how!"

"Atlas! Stop! That's the wrong way. Turn slightly to your right. Yes, yes! Now go straight!"

Jones was confused. She could hear her sister, and the way

Autumn was speaking it was almost as though Atlas could hear her too. But Jones knew that was impossible She was the only one who could hear Autumn. Right?

"Keep going! You're almost there!"

"Keep walking!" It was a new voice. It was Atlas. He must be close. But who was he talking to? Himself?

"Yes, yes, the car's just in front of you!"

Jones glanced at Hugo's ute and realised this was the car Autumn meant.

"For god sake, move your feet!" yelled Atlas.

And then she could see him, appearing through the black smoke. He had his arm around Quinn's waist and her arm was over his shoulder. Atlas was almost carrying her.

Jones raced over to help, as she heard the rumble of a vehicle behind them.

"Quick get her in the car," said Jones.

She grabbed Quinn's other arm, and pulled them towards the ute, just as Christopher's police car pulled up.

"Bring her over here!" he waved, jumping out and yanking open the door to his back seats. Hugo had also leapt out the the car, and he took over from both Jones and Atlas. Jones turned to look at Atlas and realised he was looking rather pale.

"Atlas, get in the ute. I'll get you out of here," said Jones.

Atlas slid into the passenger seat and they slammed their doors shut against the smoke. Autumn shot into the back seat just as Jones pulled the parking brake off. She quickly turned around, narrowly avoiding Christopher as he went to stop her. As she drove past he just shook his head and watched her drive away.

They bumped along the road for a few minutes before Jones's phone rang. It was Hugo.

"Jones, I'm with Wren. We're driving Quinn's car," he explained. "Christopher has called for ambulances. He says to keep driving along Ridge Top Road and then stop at the corner of Jarmyn Road. Everyone will meet us there."

"Thanks, Hugo," she said.

"Are you ok?" he asked. "Is Atlas ok?"

"I'm fine!" Atlas piped up, his voice rough, causing Hugo to let out a laugh.

"We're fine Hugo," said Jones. "Although I doubt Atlas is as fine as he thinks. But at least he's no longer at risk of going to jail."

"Too right!" Atlas said, before falling into a coughing fit. Jones reached for a water bottle in the car door and handed it to him.

"We'll see you in a minute, Hugo," said Jones.

"Good work Jones," said Hugo before hanging up.

"Can you believe it's over," said Atlas, once he had recovered and emptied the water bottle.

"No I can't," said Jones.

"And it was Quinn all along. How crazy is that!"

"I honestly can't believe it," she said.

They were silent for a few minutes, Atlas having keyed in Hugo's directions into the navigation system. Once they had turned onto Ridge Top Road and the smoke had cleared somewhat, Atlas spoke again.

"That was amazing Jones," he said quietly. "How did you do that? How did you know which way to tell us to go?"

Jones glanced into the rear vision mirror, Autumn smiling from the back seat.

"I'll tell you one day Atlas," she said, spotting the flashing lights of ambulances in the distance. "For now, let's get you checked out."

Atlas leaned his head back against the car seat and closed his eyes.

CHAPTER 39

That evening a crowd of Lilly Pilly Creek residents, along with the CFS, found themselves inside Hugo's. It was still too smoky outside to sit in the garden, but it was a pleasant atmosphere inside. The day had cooled dramatically, and the word was that although they weren't out of the woods, it was moving to containment. They just needed to ensure no fires broke the lines.

Jones sat at the bar with Wren, Mirri and Atlas. The paramedics had wanted to take him to hospital but Atlas had refused. He'd had enough of being locked up, and in his mind, the hospital was almost as bad a cell. He had promised to head in if he had even the slightest difficulty with his breathing.

They'd invited Christopher of course but he had a lot of paperwork to do and it might be days before he could relax with a beer.

"So, I've spoken to Quinn's editor," said Jones. "Sounds like she had been going rogue quite a bit recently. She was on the brink of losing her job before she got the cover story."

"Really?" said Wren, taking a sip from her white wine. "So all of this was about keeping her job?"

"And some undiagnosed mental health issues I'm guessing," said Hugo.

Jones nodded. "If it wasn't all so awful, and the fact she was more than happy for Atlas to take the fall, it would be quite sad."

The group nodded and sipped their drinks. Jones swivelled on her stool and looked out over the bar. In that room were people who had all been impacted by the bushfires. Some had lost buildings and stock. One family she knew had lost their home. The entire town had come under threat, and it would be days or even weeks before all the power, water and roads were back to functioning normally. Iris Cartwright had already started a collection tin to help the affected families on behalf of the Progress Association, and she had also asked Jones if people could drop donations into The Memory Bank for the next few days, to help anyone who needed water, clothes, stock feed or anything else that would get them back on their feet.

All the CFS women and men were getting free drinks from everyone. The whole of Lilly Pilly Creek knew they had saved the day and the town. Prue was selling car window stickers thanking the CFS, with all funds being donated to them. Jones had already spotted a few on rear windows as they drove back into town.

"But there's one thing I don't get," said Hugo. "Atlas, how did you manage to get Quinn to safety? You couldn't see a thing, could you?"

"It was Jones," said Atlas. "She was calling out, giving me directions."

Wren and Hugo turned to Jones, confused expressions on their faces.

"What, are you magic or something?" Wren said.

Jones saw Autumn perched on the counter behind Hugo. What was she supposed to say? No, actually it was Autumn's ghost who guided Atlas?

"I think you were hearing things, Atlas," said Jones. "Or maybe it was your guardian angel. I was just calling your name, calling you towards me. That was all."

"But I heard directions!" Atlas insisted. "I heard your voice giving me directions."

Jones shrugged. "What can I say? Strange things happen in emergencies." She took this opportunity to make a move. "I'm going to head back to The Memory Bank. I need to get things back in order. I think it's going to be a busy day tomorrow, what with all the donations Iris is excepting."

She said her goodbyes and Jones walked out with Hugo. Autumn floated ahead.

"It's still smoky, but it certainly feels a lot cooler," said Jones, leaning into Hugo.

Hugo put his hand out, palm up. "Hmmm, I could be mistaken, but do you feel rain?"

Jones stuck her own hand out, closing her eyes, waiting. And then she felt it. One big drop right in the centre of her palm. "Yes!" Then another and another until they both stared up into the sky. It was raining!

The pair twirled, laughing, turning their faces up to the rain. Jones imagined streaks of dust were running down her face, but she couldn't care less. Not only was the culprit caught, but the rains had come. Maybe this really was all over.

"Are you still heading off?" Hugo asked.

"Yes," said Jones. "I really must, no matter how much I'd like to stand in this rain."

Hugo kissed her. "I understand. I'll go back in and let everyone know the rains have come. Shall I come over tonight?"

Jones looked into his eyes, before pulling him into a hug. "Yes, please."

They kissed again, before Hugo, a smile on his face, walked back into the bar. "It's bloody raining!" she heard him yell.

Jones smiled, shaking her head, before looking up to see Autumn waiting for her at the door to The Memory Bank.

"He heard you, Autumn!" Jones said as she raced up to her sister. "How? I thought I was the only one who could hear you?" She fumbled with the key to The Memory Bank before finally getting the door open.

"I have absolutely no idea!" said Autumn. "I just started calling out, desperate. I didn't think it would do anything. I felt completely useless, being able to see where they were and not being able to do a thing. I was about to fly back to you, and then he replied."

"I mean, there have been moments when we've thought people have sensed you, right?" said Jones.

"Yes. Didn't you think Plum had felt me once?"

Jones nodded. "And I think Atlas has noticed you. But if he could hear you, if anyone could hear you, I'm sure we would have realised by now. Surely?"

"It is so bizarre," said Autumn. "But me being a ghost is bizarre so I'm not sure we really should be surprised."

"It's all about energy I guess," said Jones. "Perhaps the energy of the fire did something? I haven't heard you mention feeling low in recent days."

Autumn looked up at the ceiling, thinking. "You could be right. Maybe the flames give me energy. Or did the energy of the town all pulling together do something?"

"We've got so much to learn," said Jones. "Whatever happened, without your help today, I hate to think what could have happened to Atlas."

Autumn smiled, glittering tears appearing in her eyes. "I've felt so helpless the last few days. You were able to help so many people, let them in The Memory Bank, and support Atlas through this whole ordeal. But I've been floating here, with nothing I could do. When Atlas heard my voice, I realised I could finally do some good."

"Oh Autumn," said Jones "I hate that you felt that way. You are helpful in so many ways. You keep me calm, you support me when I don't know what to do. Just because you can't physically lift a box of water or talk to Atlas's family, doesn't mean you aren't helpful."

"I guess I just have to take my moment when I can. Just be at your side, ready and waiting," said Autumn.

"How lucky am I to have a ghost by my side!"

The sisters beamed at each other. After a traumatic week, they knew how lucky they truly were.

ABOUT THE AUTHOR

Abbie L. Martin is a South Australian author who lives with her family in a small town very similar to Lilly Pilly Creek. She has been dreaming of writing and publishing since she was a child, and when she reached her forties, finally decided to take the leap. Whilst also running a business with her husband, and juggling life with three children, Abbie loves nothing better than peace and quiet with a good book and a glass of wine, preferably an Adelaide Hills sparkling.

BY ABBIE L. MARTIN

The Lilly Pilly Creek Ghost Mystery Series

Book 1 - The Ghost of Lilly Pilly Creek

Book 2 - The Bride of Lilly Pilly Creek

Book 3 - The Lights of Lilly Pilly Creek

Book 4 - The Flames of Lilly Pilly Creek

www.ingramcontent.com/pod-product-compliance
Lightning Source LLC
Chambersburg PA
CBHW070554120726
47909CB00007B/2343